# WHEN THE STARS FELL

DIANE LEE BARON

When the Stars Fell

Laughing Rabbit Productions
Cover art by The Dust Jacket Designs
ISBN-13: 979-8-9879711-9-2

# *CHAPTER 1*

Andie sat on the bed, her back against the headboard, with a few small pillows wedged in for comfort. Her nightlight on the dresser beside her cast just enough light to read but still left the room in cozy darkness. She wore an over-sized tee shirt with the word Resist printed boldly on the front. It was a leftover from a woman's march in Washington, D.C. that she'd attended the previous year. In her hands she held her worn paperback copy of **Dandelion Wine**, a first edition Ray Bradbury novel. It was her favorite book, and she read it at least once a year to remind herself that the beauty of life was in the small things and in the trying. The novel had its scary parts, sure, but they were there to balance the other stories, just as in life the good lived side by side with the bad.

Andie glanced at her digital clock on the nightstand and sighed. Ten o'clock on a Friday night. She was happy enough alone in her apartment with her books to keep her company. Still, she felt it would have been nice to have been somewhere with one of her friends who lived in the area. She wondered, as she did from time to time, if she was too reclusive, too reliant on her own tendencies to keep herself occupied and content.

Andie stared at her face in the mirror above her dresser. She was average-looking with her brown eyes and pale blonde hair, her cheekbones rounded from too many Snickers bars and not enough exercise. But she knew she was pretty enough to attract other nerds that attended the science fiction conventions she loved.

Andie disliked the noise and the crowds of the local bars and restaurants found in her suburban town of Columbia, Maryland. She preferred conversations in quiet places, with thoughtful intelligent people who had a sense of humor about themselves and the world. It was no mystery to her why she rarely found a companion for any significant length of time in her hometown. Her expectations were set too high, and her tolerance for social game play was nonexistent. She was a genuine nerd, she told herself, as she twisted her blonde hair into two unsecured braids. She was a thirty-five-year-old nerd with no one to keep her from her books. A boom of thunder slightly rattled the windows. She looked up but didn't recall seeing the advance flash of lightning. Maybe it was an accident on the main road. Young guys in their flashy cars were constantly screeching through the backroads of her town, and fender benders were not unusual.

Just as Andie turned another page in the Bradbury novel, she thought she heard a noise outside, in the hallway of her apartment building. There were several voices, maybe people returning from a night out, or maybe just leaving to go somewhere. It wasn't unheard of to head out to a party or a bar in the metro area at this hour. Andie slid further down into her pillows.

Perhaps an hour or so later, she didn't take the time to check the clock, she heard a blast of a car horn, and a woman's piercing scream. Andie tossed the book onto her quilt and jumped up. Racing barefoot out of her bedroom and across the living room floor, she noticed bright lights streaming through the slats in her ceiling-to-floor window blinds. She tried looking out the peephole of her door, but couldn't make out any distinct shapes or figures. Meanwhile, the noise level outside increased with more voices and footsteps on the stairs leading to the higher apartments. She unlocked the chain and slowly opened the door several inches. She saw neighbors running throughout the apartment complex, and others standing in clusters and gesticulating wildly.

Was it a fire? A robbery? Andie couldn't make sense of the chaos. She slammed her door shut and ran back to the bedroom to toss on her underwear, jeans and a shirt. She slid her wallet into her pants' pocket, thinking that maybe the area was being evacuated due to some chemical spill or other disaster. She locked the apartment and ran outside to join the neighbors.

She approached a group of older women, and spotted Miss Bey who lived on the main floor and down the hall of Andie's building. Andie quietly entered their group, and asked, "What's going on?"

"Lordy, girl!" said Miss Bey. "Where you been at? It's all over the news."

"I've been in the apartment, reading," Andie replied.

"It's the Martians!" shouted Miss Bey. "They have landed!" The other women in the group nodded their heads in agreement and began sharing their pieces of information. "Loads of spaceships, all over the country." "No, all over the world!" "They crashed into some buildings!" "National Guard has been called up." "The President says we have to be calm, but he's gone into hiding himself!"

Andie stepped away from the agitated ladies and headed down the sidewalk to the street. Cars were parked at all angles in front of apartment buildings as tenants filled trunks and back seats with belongings and wailing children. It was large-scale panic with no apparent order to the frenzy. Andie turned in a slow circle, disbelieving the chaos taking place before her. A woman was screaming at her young daughter who clutched a ragged teddy bear and sucked on a dirty thumb. Tears of confusion ran down the child's face. Just a few feet away, two men tried to shove boxes into the back of their sport utility vehicle and only succeeded in ripping the sides of the boxes open, letting silverware and other valuables spill onto the parking lot.

Andie noticed one of the apartment maintenance workers, a trustworthy and friendly man, and his wife dragging trash bags of belongings to their car. "Ricardo!" she called. "Where are you going? What are you doing?"

Ricardo stopped dragging his bags to face Andie, sweat pouring down his face and his breath coming in wheezing gasps, "I'm getting out of here. I'm not hanging around to see what those green men are gonna do to us. Anyone who stays is a fool. I've seen those movies, and it never comes out right for the people. No sirree, me and Gracie are outta here." He turned away from Andie and continued lugging his bags. "You should go, too, Ms. Thompson. While there's time!" Ricardo called back.

Andie stepped onto the lawn, away from the cars. Her head spun from the sparse yet shocking information she'd just heard. Aliens, here, on Earth. It was madness. There was no other life outside in the universe; Carl Sagan had proven it decades ago. The chances were too remote; the variables were insurmountable. Surely, this was all a hoax, some War of the Worlds hoax.

She heard the partial whoop-whoop of a police car alarm and turned to see lights flashing amid the car jam in front of her. She pushed through a crowd of people and made her way to the officer, still seated in his vehicle with his windows open. She leaned over and called through the window. "What the hell is going on, officer? No one's making any sense. Are there really aliens?"

The young officer shook his head with his lips pressed tightly together. Andie could see that he needed to get through the traffic jam but he was stuck and heading nowhere fast. "Please," she begged. "I just need to know."

The officer turned to her, and she could clearly see anxiety run across his swarthy handsome features. "Listen," he said. "We have a real emergency going on, and not just here. It's everywhere. Flying saucers or whatever they are landed all over the country around nine o'clock this evening." He paused to take a deep breath. "It has hit the fan, if you know what I mean."

The officer looked out the front window at the chaos in her neighborhood then ran his hand nervously through his dark wavy hair. "I need to get through this traffic and over to Lake Elkhorn. The dispatcher just radioed me that one of the UFOs landed there."

Andie's heart skipped a beat, and her voice raised several octaves. "Right here? In Columbia? But why?"

"Lady, your guess is as good as mine. But I have to follow orders, and I have to do it right now!" The officer kept scanning the crowds for a way to drive safely through.

"Okay. Okay. How about if I direct the cars for you? Maybe you could let me come along with you to Lake Elkhorn? I have a car in the closed garage over there," she said as she pointed to one of several single unit parking garages, "but there's no way I'll be able to get it out in this mess."

The police officer hesitated.

"Come on. Who's to know? This is an emergency, and nobody will be paying any attention." Andie didn't wait for his response but ran over to several neighbors who were loading their cars with children, pillows, and bags of assorted foods and valuables.

"Hello? Listen, I need you to pull up your cars on to the grass. The cop needs to get through. He's got to go, um, somewhere else where he's needed badly. There are people in danger. Let's help out our good guys." Andie pleaded, hoping to somehow appeal to the compassion in her neighbors.

One cooperative woman jumped into her car and lurched it over the curb and forward onto the grass, cutting down a shrub in the process. Andie signaled the woman with a thumbs up.

"Thank you!" she called over the din. She turned to the next car in the middle of the road.

"Please, sir, help us. Move your car over!" She stood in front of a large, balding man with a beer belly, her hands out in supplication.

The man shook his head in a sharp negative movement and ran around Andie and back towards the apartment building to retrieve more belongings. Andie sprinted to his over-sized sport utility vehicle and looked inside. She was in luck. The keys were in the ignition. She grabbed the door and swung herself into the car. She turned the key to start the car then slammed on the pedal to drive the car forward on to another section of the lawn. The SUV's owner came down the apartment breezeway with arms full of clothing, his eyes popping in his fleshy face and his jaws wide open in shock. He ran toward the car, dropping pairs of pants, belts and pocket change all over the sidewalk. His fury was a heat-seeking missile, with Andie as his target.

Andie bolted from the SUV and sprinted as fast as her legs could carry her towards the police car. She pulled at the passenger door but received a painful jolt to her arm when it refused to open. The door was locked. "Open the door! Hey, he's going to kill me. I did my part, now you do yours!" She made focused eye contact with the officer.

Andie heard the unlocking of the door and pulled it hard and fast. She slid into the front seat next to the police officer, then slammed her door. "Now lock it! Lock it!" she screamed. Just in time, the door locks were set, and the SUV owner was left pounding on the roof. The police officer rammed the gas pedal, and Andie felt her head bounce off the cushions of the seat. The irate man jumped back as the police car pushed forward. The car barely made the passage through two other parked vehicles, but soon they were free of the wild melee and heading down the apartment complex drive at breakneck speed.

# CHAPTER 2

"I didn't say that I'd let you ride along with me! You just went ahead and put yourself in an incredibly dangerous situation. I should have left you out there to defend yourself. You're a crazy person." The police officer muttered as he negotiated the packed roads leading to the major Baltimore/Washington highways. He passed the Route 32 entrance in a flash.

"You're welcome," Andie responded. "Sheesh. You'd think a person would be grateful for some assistance, even if it did end up a bit messy." She mumbled this under her breath as she stared out the window, noticing bright lights illuminating the dark evening sky a few miles ahead. She figured that the lights were at the alien landing site. It would be a media field day, not to mention all the spectators and police and emergency presence. Of course, that's *if* there was an actual landing, she thought. She was still feeling skeptical.

"Messy? It was insane." The officer clenched both his jaw and the steering wheel.

Andie felt herself regaining her regular breathing at the same time as the ridiculousness of the situation overwhelmed her. She started laughing and found it hard to stop. She was usually level-headed, unless circumstances were unusual. Like the time she served a vegan meal to a male friend, and because he wasn't used to large amounts of beans, he'd spent the evening in the bathroom. She'd been rather giggly then, too. Between gasps for air, Andie turned to the cop and asked, "Did you see how red that guy's face was? I thought he was going to explode."

The cop's lips turned upwards in a half-smile. "I kind of thought having his jockeys all over the sidewalk was rather amusing."

Andie took the policeman's comment to mean he was feeling less angry at her and more willing to accept her overture for friendship. "Hi, I'm Andie Thompson, your date for the space invasion."

The officer spared a quick glance at Andie, then shook his head. "The name's Frank. Lieutenant Frank Terranova of the Howard County Police Department."

"Pleased to meet you, Officer Frank. And thank-you for the lift. I would have had to walk over to Lake Elkhorn, and it's a few miles from my apartment."

"I don't know what we're going to find at the lake, but whatever it is has my supervisors nervous. There's been an all-call for everyone in the area. I bet it's another landing site. I've heard a spaceship landed near Philly. There's a ton of others in states all over the country."

"This is so creepy and unbelievable."

"I've got to say that I'm a bit anxious. They didn't train us for alien invasions at the academy. Here we go," said Officer Terranova. He slowed down as he approached the parkland in front of the lake. "All the parking is filled. We'll have to pull over by the dam. It's going to be bumpy." The car banged over the cement curb and headed downhill towards a gazebo. Elkhorn Park was packed with emergency vehicles with lights flashing, a few sirens wailing and the sound of car radios relaying information. Andie and Frank sat still for a moment, gawking at the astonishing display.

"Wow," Andie remarked. "Now this is a major mess."

"Yeah. Only much worse than what you did back at the apartment complex," Frank smiled at Andie. "Well, time to get to work." He opened his door, leaving his car lights and radio on. Andie got out of the car and started to follow Officer Frank. He was already striding towards the crowds of policeman grouped up by the roadway.

*Huh. Some date,* she said to herself as she walked with others who were headed in the opposite direction to the lake.

A perimeter of police tape surrounded the front portion of the lake to hold back the gawking crowds. Lights on scaffolds were set up at regular intervals and illuminated a large portion of the lake and the pathways around it, but did not illuminate the strange object that sat in the lake. There was a spaceship, or so it seemed, almost filling the lake. It rested at a slight angle upwards towards the townhouse side of the lake. Since the manmade lake was only about eight feet deep, Andie estimated that the circular ship was 50 feet across. Its black hull was dense with darkness. No areas reflected the light. Instead, the ship seemed to be a black void, apart from its surroundings and yet within them. The spaceship appeared to be seamless, with no apparent windows or doorways.

Andie observed the crowds of people who had come out of curiosity, just like her. It seemed rather unusual to her that some people were fleeing Columbia while others were staying to view the novelty of the spaceship. People were attempting to take photos of the craft with their phones, but Andie was pretty sure that the resulting photos would be disappointing due to the nature of the ship's surface and the press of the evening sky. Many officers patrolled the lakeside to keep people at a distance from the ship, their guns visible in their holsters, but the majority of the police presence remained a hub of activity closer to the street. Andie was positioned on the side of the lake farthest from the spaceship and was slightly comforted by this distance.

Andie walked towards the dock that reached out about 20 feet over the water. Several people were on the dock, leaning over, trying to get a better view. Andie walked a few yards past the dock, and then stood in a relatively quiet area among trees that encroached on the water's edge. She was frightened, wondering what would happen next. Her survival instincts were telling her that something would happen, that something had to happen. But the strange thing was that the supposed spaceship wasn't very big, not for a spacefaring vehicle. Were there small intelligent beings inside? The one thing that Andie was sure of was that whomever or whatever sent the spaceships down to Earth had to have a reason for doing so. *Dear Heavens,* she thought, *please don't let this be like Grover's Corners.*

Besides the sounds of the emergency cars and the occasional shouts from people, Andie realized that she heard no animals. Usually, she was greeted with the sounds of birds, cicadas, the rustling of squirrels in the trees. Of course, this was nighttime, but still, it seemed that nature was being quiet. Perhaps it was watching and waiting like she was. Just then, she saw the glistening of a frog on the dirt edge of the water. It was only a few feet away. She saw the throat extend and retract, but no sound came. Then she watched as the frog took one leap and jumped into the lake water with a small splash. She expected to see the frog's head emerge, but that didn't happen. Instead, she saw the frog's body come to the water's surface, lying on its back and arms splayed apart from the body. Within seconds, the skin of the frog peeled away revealing the muscles. And then that too peeled away and all that was left were the bones, a cartilage outline of the once- living frog. The bones stayed intact for longer than the skin and muscles, the softer tissues, but then they too dissolved. Within two minutes, all evidence of the frog was gone, eaten away by the water. No, Andie thought. What was *in* the water had caused this. The spaceship was releasing something terrible and lethal into Lake Elkhorn, and if it could cause the death of a frog, it could kill people, too.

Andie ran back towards the crowds of police and emergency staff. She struggled with her breathing and cursed herself for not being as fit as she wanted to be. It seemed even harder to get where she wanted to go, knowing that her information was imperative for the safety of others. She ran through the sea of black and blue clothed officers, madly searching for a familiar face, someone who would believe her dire news. "Frank," she yelled, as she spotted the police officer. "Officer Terranova! I have to tell you something!"

Frank turned away from his colleagues who were listening to a radio broadcast from one of the police cars. "Andie," he said in recognition.

Andie grabbed his sleeve. "It's important that you tell everyone! Don't let people near the water. It's poisoned. I saw it melt a frog in seconds, bones and all! Who knows what it would do to a person!"

"Is that right?" Frank asked. "You saw it yourself?"

"Yes! Over by the dock. I watched the frog jump in, and the water just stripped it of its skin and bones. Please tell me you believe me!" She pleaded with him as tears threatened to spill.

Frank looked at Andie solemnly for a few seconds, nodded once then he turned on his heels and ran to his commanding officer. It was clear that Andie's information was being shared because immediately more officers headed towards the lake side and the growing sea of people.

Andie wrapped her arms around herself, shivering from cold and fear. How could they handle things if the aliens wanted to kill people as easily as they had killed the frog?

# *CHAPTER 3*

Andie had no intention of staying at Lake Elkhorn. It was too unsettling, too strange. She knew that she had to make plans and make them fast. She needed to protect herself in the event of some future catastrophe. She wasn't a survivalist, but she did believe she needed to be prepared for the worst. In the darkness she jogged then racewalked the two miles back towards her apartment complex. Where sidewalks ended, she ran on the main roads or on the islands between lanes. She was honked at, and sworn at, but she didn't care. She had to stop often to catch her breath. 'Think,' she told herself. 'Come up with a plan.' She was dazed by the confusion of car lights, by the image of the dark saucer in the lake, by the innocent frog being flayed alive layer by layer.

When she came to the T-stop in the road, she made a quick decision to turn right towards the shopping center instead of heading left towards home. Surprisingly, the 24- hour shopping center wasn't busy. She had expected hordes of panicked shoppers descending on the grocery store, as they did during other emergency situations such as snow storms and hurricanes, stocking up on toilet paper and milk.

Andie had a mission. She decided to supply her apartment and hunker down to figure out her next move during this weird time. She grabbed a large grocery cart inside the store, and headed towards the canned food aisle. She tossed cans of tuna fish, soup, beans, canned fruits, and other durable consumables into the cart. She didn't want to take any chances in case electricity was compromised in some way. She shoved large water bottles on the bottom rungs of the cart. She grabbed batteries and matches; she had plenty of flashlights and candles at home. She grabbed chocolate bars and a package of Oreos because it was her go-to stress food. She also took some Tylenol boxes, toothpaste, shampoo and, because it was an emergency, rolls of toilet paper. She felt like she was a contestant on Supermarket Sweeps as she zipped up and down the aisles. She joined other wild-eyed shoppers in line at the cashier and tried to think of anything she might have missed. She looked at the glossy covers of the popular magazines. It was only a few hours ago that the faces on these magazine covers might have mattered to someone. Now, life on Earth had changed.

Andie paid for the purchases in her crammed cart with her debit card and pushed the cart through the doors and into the night. Right outside the store, there were pallets where a few potted azaleas remained. A plastic tarp lay rolled up on the pavement beside the pallets. In a swift and instinctual decision, Andie grabbed the black tarp and tucked it around and into the grocery cart, effectively covering all the items. With her car at home and no immediate means of transporting her groceries, Andie began to push the cart towards home. It was a quarter mile to the apartment, with a good portion of the trip uphill. Andie struggled as she pushed the cart inch by inch, sometimes using her whole body against the cart. She hurt from head to toe and sweat fell from her forehead to obscure her vision. She was petrified that someone would stop her because she had a stolen cart, or worse, because she had a cart full of food and supplies. She tried to stay near trees and away from the streetlight. At one point some teenagers yelled at her from out their car windows and she felt a jerk of fear, but they didn't stop and neither did she. More than once she wished she'd gone home first and gotten her car for this mission, but it was too late for self- recriminations.

Andie pushed the cart up the final short but steep hill into the apartment complex. The road went flat, and she stopped to calm her wildly beating heart. The apartment buildings were now mostly quiet, with only several cars dotting the parking lots and a few lights shining in windows. Andie felt relieved by the exodus and the subsequent emptiness. The noise and clamor were gone, leaving only an uneasy peace. Andie gathered her courage about her. She was home now, and she would deal with whatever situation arose by herself. She was strong, and best of all, she was resilient. The cart banged over the uneven sidewalk and finally she was in front of her building. She headed down the short breezeway to her apartment, when the door to Miss Bey's apartment banged open.

"You still here?" Miss Bey asked. She was in her long nightgown with curlers in her wiry hair. She had removed her dentures, so her words were slurred as she moved her lips over her gums.

Andie stopped and smiled. She had always had a soft spot for Miss Bey, an elderly former minister of a Protestant church.

"I am," Andie said. "I thought you were taking off with Ricardo and the others."

"Ah, no. I ain't leaving my home and all my things for some flying saucer. I'm staying right here, and everybody can do what they want and leave me be. And that means any Martians, too."

Andie smiled at her incorrigible neighbor. "Okay, Miss Bey. But if you have any trouble or you need anything, you come and see me, okay? I just picked up some food and things at the store in case things get a bit wacky." Miss Bey was a gentle soul who sometimes mistakenly picked up large amounts of groceries like corn or milk and then shared them with Andie.

Miss Bey laughed. "Wacky, huh? I think I done seen wacky in my time, and I can deal with it, let me tell you." She smacked her lips together, as if relishing the prospect of more craziness to come.

"Okay, Miss Bey. Then I'll check on you now and then."

"You do that. Night, now," she said, closing the door.

Andie pushed the cart the remaining feet down the hallway, fished her house keys from her pocket, and unlocked her door. Her apartment looked so familiar, so normal, that she almost wept with gratitude. She couldn't push the grocery cart through the narrow doorway, so she offloaded all the purchases into her dining room just inside. Andie rolled the cart back outside and on to the front lawn of her building. She would take it back to the store in the morning, or sometime soon.

Back in her apartment, she shoved the few perishable groceries like milk into the fridge then fell into her recliner and closed her eyes. Her nerves might have kept her awake if her sheer exhaustion hadn't taken hold and carried her off into a deep sleep. Andie's dark dreams were woven with images of SUVs that chased her and ferocious dogs that nipped at her heels as she ran. The despairing cries she made in her dreams went unheard by aliens or the few other residents left in her building as she tried to save herself from her nightmares.

# *CHAPTER 4*

Andie awoke midmorning, relieved to see that the electricity was on. She'd only slept a few hours but she felt alert. She took a long soothing shower, then returned to her recliner with a hot Earl Grey tea in hand in order to view the news. Sure enough, the alien invasion was on every major station. Frantic newscasters, bleary-eyed and disheveled, spoke in catastrophic phrases and let it be known that no one was safe. Never mind that nothing had happened, except that several hundred ships had landed all over the Earth near major cities. Andie surmised that Columbia was selected due to its proximity to D.C. and Baltimore. Mayors and governors of cities encouraged citizens to remain in their homes, but the major highways throughout the United States proved that many people were on the move. Easterners went West, Northerners went South and there seemed to be no rhyme or reason to the exodus. Andie felt reassured that she had made a good decision, if only for today. No word was to be had from the President of the United States, but that surprised no one. It was better that this president remain in his bunker and stay out of the way of the people who could deal firsthand with this situation. The local emergency personnel would soon be relieved by the Army and the National Guard in the crisis areas of the United States. It had been less than 24 hours, and the country was marshalling forces to handle the alien situation.

After several hours of watching the news, Andie grew tired of the repetition, with the talking heads and so-called experts from alien conspiracy groups droning on with no new details to add to the story. In the late afternoon she dressed and decided to go for a walk around the apartment complex. She needed fresh air and a way to stretch her aching muscles from yesterday's exertions. The Air Force and local weather helicopters had done aerial surveillance and determined that there had been no further movement from the spaceships. She was tempted to walk over to Lake Elkhorn but felt that sticking close to home was the safest bet at this time. The complex was quiet without the usual high schoolers pounding basketballs on the pavement and the younger children whirring their bicycle wheels down the road. No children of any age could be seen or heard. She walked the familiar sidewalk, passing the closed and locked rental office. Very few cars were travelling on Murray Road in front of the complex, and the deli down the street was dark and closed.

Andie had almost completed the circle around the apartment complex when she unexpectedly heard a soft bark behind her. She swirled around to come face to face with a tall young man and his bulldog standing a few feet away.

"Oh!" she cried. She clutched at her shirt with her left hand, her right hand held fisted in order to defend herself.

"Sorry! Sorry!" the man said to her. "We didn't mean to scare you. We were just out for a walk." His kind and attractive face was filled with concern.

"Geez!" She took a deep breath. "You didn't have to sneak up on me like that. Next time make some noise, like a few yards away."

The lean young man looked to be about thirty and had thick brown hair and green eyes. "Okay, no problem. And perhaps I should whistle, too. Or sing a few bars of something rock and roll?"

He was trying to put Andie at ease, and his winning smile went a long way in doing so.

Andie responded by letting down her guard. "Only if that ugly dog sings baritone."

"He can do that. But don't call him ugly." The guy looked serious. His green eyes flashed at Andie's insult.

Andie looked down at the dog who now lay on the pavement in the warm sun. "He sort of is." The bulldog had taken the opportunity for a short siesta as his owner talked to Andie.

"Shh! He'll hear you. He's very sensitive about his looks."

"Uh-huh. That's why he's licking his privates right now," Andie said.

"Everyone expresses themselves in different ways."

"Ha!" Andie laughed. "Okay, I guess you win. I'm Andie Thompson."

"And I'm Joseph Jameson, but you can call me Joe." The man reached out to shake Andie's hand.

"Joe Cool?"

The handsome man rolled his eyes, and he took a deep breath. "It's just Joe, okay? Just regular old Joe."

"I'm sorry, I was teasing." Andie didn't want to get off on the wrong foot with this guy. She'd been keeping the conversation light, or so she thought, but she had to remember that not every one had her quirky sense of humor.

"Never mind. And this is my dog, Satchmo." He indicated down on the sidewalk where the bulldog had resumed soaking up the last warmth of the waning sun. Evening was coming soon.

"Satchmo. I get it. Because he has those big fat cheeks." Andie was glad to see Joe nodding. "Well, Joe. Why are you here? I mean, why did you stay? Most people got the hell out of Dodge last night."

"Probably for the same reason as you, I suppose," Joe said. "It's home, and who knows what to do, really?"

"Yes, that's true. I'm just roosting here and waiting for some clue on what comes next." Andie breathed deeply again, seeking to calm herself.

"Have you been down to the lake?" Joe asked. He looked in the direction of Lake Elkhorn.

"Yes, last night." She reached up to pull her hair back off her face.

"I rode my bike over a few hours ago. I have to say it was incredible to see something I've wanted to see all my life." Joe looked thrilled at the memory. "I'm the biggest science fiction fan ever. When I was a kid, I used to look up at the nighttime sky and literally pray for aliens to come to earth."

"Not the probing kind?"

"Hell, no. Just the sweet big-headed kind from the Close Encounters movie."

Andie smiled and nodded in agreement. "That would be awesome. I guess we'll have to wait and see. Oh, and I'm a big science fiction fan, too." She watched as Joe leaned down to rub Satchmo's head.

"Maybe I could borrow your bike later and check it out again?" Andie's curiosity was overriding her fears. "It's too crowded over there for my car."

"No problem. I ..." Then suddenly, Joe whipped his head around, as if searching for something. "Shh! Listen!" He held his hand up to caution her.

"What?" she whispered. It was then she spotted it. Something black, something unknown, flying towards them from a block away. Andie froze in place. This wasn't a drone; this was something else. Just then a squirrel in a tree a few feet away from the flying object scampered up the trunk. The object stopped dead and swirled towards the squirrel. An aperture opened, but just as quickly closed.

As this happened, Joe picked up Satchmo and pulled Andie towards the covered garbage shed close to her apartment. He closed the door. leaving just a half-inch open for him to look out. Andie peered around Joe's shoulders, trying to gain a glimpse of the flying object. Satchmo resumed napping in Joe's arms.

The object stayed facing the squirrel for a few seconds then turned towards the place Joe and Andie had stood. The ovoid object flew with an odd humming sound, like nothing Andie had heard before. The object stopped where they had stood only moments ago then moved on past the shed. Andie and Joe remained stock still. Satchmo needed no warnings for silence. Joe watched the object continue on to Andie's front lawn where it stopped a few feet away from a cardinal hopping up to a higher branch in a tree then headed towards another squirrel running across the lawn at the next apartment building.

Just then a man stepped out of the foyer of the next apartment building. Within seconds and without warning, they saw the device zip over to the man. The aperture opened and a red piercing light flashed. Andie heard the man's scream, loud yet brief. The man had been disintegrated.

"Oh my god," Andie whispered. "Oh my god, it killed him!" She began to shake in place.

"Let's wait a minute. Until it's gone," Joe replied. He squeezed her shoulder then turned back to the slit in the doorway.

Several minutes later, without a sign of the suspicious object, the trio left the shed.

"I live over here," Andie pointed to her apartment. "Come on!" she urged.

They raced to Andie's apartment, each praying that the object wouldn't return. Clearly, the alien object was a killing device. If the flying thing could decimate humans, everyone, man, woman or child, was in big trouble.

# *CHAPTER 5*

Within the confines of Andie's apartment, the memories of the last few minutes outside seemed surreal. Joe walked Satchmo over to a corner of the living room, where the dog circled the carpet then plopped down. Joe then examined Andie's storehouse of foods and supplies in the dining area. "Looks like you cleaned out the supermarket," he said as he surveyed the pile of goods.

"Good thing, too," Andie said. "If that death ray thing sticks around, we may have to hide out here for a while." She shuddered and wrapped her arms around herself. "My god, that was beyond scary."

Joe turned around and surveyed the apartment. The dining room abutted the living room with the kitchen separated from the two rooms with a half wall. He walked over to the large floor to ceiling windows and inspected them. The windows were covered with long hanging blinds.

"I don't think these are going to keep us safe. If we turn on the TV or a light, we'll be seen from the outside."

Andie picked up the tarp she'd acquired at the grocery store. "How about this? It's black, and I don't think light will shine through." Joe felt the woven material of the tarp. "This is good. Do you have a hammer and nails so we can hang it over the blinds?"

"I have two hammers for some reason, and..." She looked around her living room. "We can take down my pictures and pull out the nails." She began running around the room removing her sea life pictures and stacking them against a wall. Joe pulled the nails from the walls.

"Okay," he said. "Hold this side up, and I'll hammer the tarp up." It was hard work to fit the tarp against the wall and above the window fixtures. The tarp covered the window with little to spare. They used Andie's roll of electrical tape to pull the tarp even tighter against the wall. After an hour, long after the sun had set, Andie and Joe rested on the carpet next to Satchmo, talking softly.

"I don't get it," Andie said. "Why didn't that thing come back and zap us? It passed us right by, and we even had the door open a bit."

"I've been thinking about that," Joe said. "Maybe the object is sensitive to movement. It saw us, or felt us, when we were moving on the sidewalk, but when we stood in the shed, it didn't seem to recognize us. It noticed the squirrels and the cardinal when they were moving, too."

"But it didn't attack them."

"No. Maybe the objects have a schematic of living things here on Earth. It ignores the little moving creatures but goes into attack mode when its program verifies a match with humans."

Andie looked at Joe askance. "Maybe," she said. "So, what you're saying is that the nasty object may also have a schema of humans."

"Seems that way."

"That means that they or whatever runs them has been to Earth before. Aliens could be among us right now, and we might not even recognize them because they are in disguise or invisible."

Joe rested his head on his knees. "Anything seems possible after today."

Andie stiffened, and grabbed Joe's wrist. "It's coming! I hear it!"

They both listened to the humming sound of the flying object as it travelled down the breezeway outside of Andie's apartment. Satchmo, awoken either from Andie's excited words or from the buzzing from outdoors, lifted his head, then barked. Andie and Joe froze. But the device kept on moving and finally could be heard no more.

"It seems that it's not programmed to respond to sound, either," Andie whispered.

"So, I guess we don't have to whisper, now do we?" Joe teased with a slight smile. Andie turned to Joe, ready to admonish him for being glib during such a tense time, but then she realized he was trying to lighten the tension. She appreciated that. A lot.

"Let's turn on the TV," Andie suggested. "We can cover the reflections of the screen with towels or sheets just to be safe and listen to the news."

"Or we could cover the screen with a quilt and get under it to watch the news," Joe suggested.

"Even better," Andie said.

After they fixed the TV with quilts and folding chairs, they sat next to each other, munching on Oreos and viewing the horrors that were occurring in other parts of the country. Again and again, newscasters reported sightings of the black flying deadly objects that cremated humans indiscriminately. Orders were given for people to take cover inside and to stay away from the windows. Many people had been killed by peeking out their windows or doors. Of course, many others had lost their lives in cold blood as they unsuspectedly moved about in the early evening before the knowledge of the armed objects was known. Military drones sent to spy on the objects determined that the discs were moving methodically through neighborhoods and towns. Eventually no one was allowed outside, by government order. Military craft were sent to destroy the objects with lasers and short-range missiles, but to no avail. The spherical objects seemed impervious to any basic weaponry. Attempts to catch the small objects failed due to their incredible agility and speed. Not to mention, it was dangerous to use most highly-powered weapons around heavily populated areas.

Because the spaceship landings and the killing objects that were presumed to have come from them were situated far apart in the major cities, there were towns that were not affected at all by the alien landings. People moved freely through the streets and stores without sightings or attacks. Rural areas were unaffected by the country's crisis, and many mountain people believed that it was all a tall tale created by the government in order to keep the people under control.

"There's something else I don't understand," Andie said as she reached inside the cookie bag that Joe held in his hands.

"What's that?" Joe mumbled through his cookie crumbs.

"Well, it seems a bit inefficient to have these machines flying around and killing only the people that move outside. I mean, there aren't a lot of them. And what's the point?"

"Maybe they're mapping out the neighborhoods and such. You know, for when their overlords come," Joe answered half joking, yet half serious.

Andie turned to face Joe. "That's just it. There has to be others. These nasty things can't be it. The spaceships that they came in surely couldn't cross a solar system on their own, could they?"

"I don't think so, Andie. But I just don't know. No one does." He met her glance with his own penetrating green eyes. "We should try to get some rest. I'll take the couch, if you don't mind."

"No, that's good." Earlier, they had rigged up a newspaper area in the bathroom for Satchmo to do his business so he wouldn't have to go outside. It had been difficult for the bulldog, but after a while he gave in to using the area. Now he was sleeping and snoring back in his corner on the carpet. Andie tossed a blanket to Joe, who caught it in one hand and placed it under his head for a pillow as he staked out the couch.

Sighing, Andie walked down the hall to her bedroom. The vertical blinds on her bedroom windows were the same type as in the living room but since she wasn't using any lamps, she felt that she was safe in her own bed. She tossed a few sheets over the fixtures of the blinds then slid into her bed. She hadn't slept in her bed in 48 hours, and it felt like heaven. The cool sheets caressed her tired body while the pillows gently cushioned her head. It was then that she heard the sound again. The sound of a death object. Outside her window. She held herself still and attempted to breathe quietly and without movement. Her back was to the window, but she closed her eyes anyway. The object continued on its relentless quest. As soon as the sound was gone, Andie crawled out of her bed and slipped to the floor. She pulled a blanket around her and continued crawling down the hallway and back to the relative safety of the living room. She collapsed at the foot of the couch, her blanket tangled around her and fell into a deep dreamless sleep.

In the morning, Andie awoke to Joe standing over her. "Hello. And to what do I owe the pleasure of your company?"

Andie rubbed her gritty eyes and yawned. "Sorry. Yes, well. A death ray thingie flew by my window last night and freaked me out. It seemed like there was safety in numbers, so I crawled back here."

"I don't blame you. I should have considered that might happen." He shook his head. "What a nightmare."

"Literally. So, what are you doing up?" Andie stood up with her blanket wrapped loosely around her.

"I'm heading back to my apartment," said Joe.

Andie frowned. This news brought her widely awake. "But why? You're safe here. So is Satchmo. How are you going to avoid the black things?"

"I turned on the news. All the flying things disappeared at dawn. No one knows where they went. But it seems that for now, it's all clear."

"I thought you'd stay…" Andie didn't mean to imply that she was afraid or incapable of taking care of herself, but she had felt somewhat safe by being with Joe. He was nice, and it helped having someone to bounce her thoughts against.

"Andie, I need to get dog food for Satchmo. People food is just too rich for him, even though he loves it. And my cellphone is back there. I have plenty of food, too." He folded his blanket and put it on the arm of the couch.

"That's fine," Andie said. "I'll be okay." She smiled although her feelings were mixed. "Stop by soon and say hi, okay?"

"Sure. Of course. You, too." He called Satchmo over to him, then turned to Andie. "If you learn anything new, let me know. Call me on the cell." He gave her his cell phone number, and she programmed the number into her phone.

"Be safe, guys." She opened the apartment door and let them pass through. Joe gave a slight wave, looking almost tentative as if he was suddenly hesitant to leave, and then he and his dog were gone. Andie closed her door and leaned against it. "Well, that was interesting," she said to the empty room.

# CHAPTER 6

Andie showered, then spent the rest of the morning cleaning and organizing her apartment. She was aware that she was using familiar routines to comfort herself. She'd always cleaned when something at work had upset her. Being a high school teacher gave her plenty of opportunities to be stressed, from grading assignments, preparing lessons, dealing with controlling parents and staying in good with the administration. And now she was cleaning because aliens had landed in her backyard. She had called in to work to see if they were opening, but it was only a formality because she knew the current circumstances would keep the schools closed. She shook her head wryly, then pulled her medium- length blonde hair into a ponytail with the use of an elastic.

She decided to organize her food stuffs in groups on the dining room table while other dry goods were neatly placed on the kitchen counters. It was a bit OCD, but she felt the need to control something in this crazy world. In the background played the streaming news services which she listened to with one ear. The flying objects had killed tens of thousands of people around the country. Instead of vaporizing the living, the black objects had actually cremated them. The evidence was found in small piles of ash and bones left where the people had stood. It was a disaster of unparalleled proportions, especially in cities like New York or Boston. The major broadcast news stations showed many pictures of formerly alive people, stopped dead in their evening activities. Some people were caught moving in their cars, and the objects had blasted through the windows to attack them. Andie choked back tears when camera footage from the first day of the attacks, before people were warned, showed a Maryland carnival with piles of ashes everywhere. Andie imagined the piles were teenagers out for a good time, or children with their parents, trying to win a stuffed animal at the coin toss booth.

It was estimated that about one thousand spaceships had landed in the United States. The space vehicles had mostly been found in shallow bodies of water near major cities with dense populations. Various science agencies speculated that the water was used as a coolant after entry through Earth's atmosphere. It was also theorized that the smaller spheres were actually formed from the body of the spaceships. The surfaces appeared similar, with their dark non-reflective impenetrable surfaces. No one had observed the small objects entering or leaving the bigger ships, so perhaps the spheres came from the actual material of the ship. Of course, none of these theories had yet to be proven.

As Andie worked in her kitchen, she came to the conclusion that she was going to leave her apartment and find somewhere safer to live. There were still many rural and mountain areas that had not been affected by the alien landings. Maybe she could get in her car and drive to one of those places. She thought of calling some nearby friends to see what they were planning, but decided that they were consumed with their own worries. She hated asking people for help at the best of times, but now that this weird apocalypse was upon them, she was even less likely to be inclined to bother friends. It was a personal flaw, she admitted to herself, but it caused her to have faith in her own strengths, for good or for bad.

When the news station put out a special bulletin that announced that astronomers at the Hubble Space Observatory had possibly spotted movements or wavering of space by Alpha Centauri that were of unknown origin and appeared to be coming towards Earth, Andie felt a cold chill run through her. Scientists hadn't figured the exact rate of travel, but it appeared that these unknown phenomena could enter our solar system within a week or two. Andie's thoughts of fleeing grew even stronger. Was it time to go, or should she wait?

Andie needed to get out of her apartment and go outside. She locked her apartment door and walked down the hallway. She knocked on Miss Bey's door, but there was no answer. Andie was sorry to miss her, but Miss Bey was probably napping. Andie continued on a walk through her apartment complex. It was eerie how things seemed so normal. The daffodils were standing tall on green stems. The robins and cardinals were darting through the trees, and the sky was a soft blue with only a few scudding clouds. It was a perfect April day.

As she passed by the next building, Andie observed a small group of people standing in a tight circle looking downwards. She gasped with horror when she realized they were praying at a small mound of dirt at their feet. She was certain it was the remains of a person. She stopped and watched for a moment, taking in the wracking sobs and heartfelt words spoken over the mound and saying her own quiet prayer. She moved on, hoping not to distract the mourners.

The death of an innocent person, perhaps the man she had heard screaming last evening, upset her, but it also made her angry. The aliens had entered her world, her neighborhood, and she wanted them gone. Whatever it took to get the things gone, she would help to do it. She was only one person, but sometimes one person could do mighty things. She would no longer be a victim, someone quivering behind her apartment door. It was time to get going and learn all she could. They said that information was power, didn't they? She would learn.

The first place to go was Lake Elkhorn. She wanted to see the alien spaceship again. She wanted to observe it at every angle. There had to be something more she could learn. Andie planned on walking to the lake, but then she spotted a bicycle hidden behind an air conditioning unit at the end of the one of the buildings. The bike was unlocked, so Andie dragged it out from behind the bushes. It would certainly make for a faster trip, even though Andie hadn't ridden on a bike in years. She wobbled a bit in the beginning but soon hit her stride as she pedaled up small hills and raced on the flat areas of the sidewalks. Her decision to not take her car turned out to be a good one, as she veered around cars that still littered the major roads. Tow trucks were working to remove the driverless cars, the cars owned by targets of the killer objects. Andie spotted a cyclist ahead of her who had stopped and was talking to a pedestrian. As Andie got closer, she saw that it was Joe on the bike. She slowed and pulled up to the men, who were deep in conversation.

"Hey, Joe," she called out. "How's it going?"

Joe turned and smiled in recognition. "Andie! What brings you out here?"

"Um, aliens. I'm headed over to see the spaceship again. How about you?"

"Same. Andie, this is Ray. He was just over at Lake Elkhorn. He says its quite a scene."

"Yeah," Ray confirmed. "There are tons of police and some military personnel over there. They've pretty much sealed off all entrances to the park, and now they're trying to figure out who the remains belong to." Ray's mouth took on a grim line. He didn't have to explain what he meant by remains. "It's not going to be easy."

"I guess those damn objects got the police and the regular joes who were just hanging around last night," Joe said.

"From what I heard and saw, that seems to be about 75 people," Ray replied.

Andie gasped, bringing her hand to her mouth.

"I was going over to see if I can help, but I guess I'd be more of a nuisance than anything," Joe said. Ray nodded and said, "Probably so."

"I'm still going," said Andie. "I just need to see the spaceship." Her heart was racing and she could barely breathe, but she was determined to continue forward.

"Well, sure, then I'll go with you," said Joe. "Thanks, Ray. Be well and be safe."

"I'm heading home to my wife, Annmarie. We're getting out of here soon. Maybe tomorrow. You two take care as well," said Ray, heading in the direction of an apartment complex situated close to the grocery store.

Andie and Joe cycled the final mile to the lake. It was impossible not to stare at the cars in the road that had been pushed to the side by other cars trying to get through. Andie tried not to look at the shattered windows that remained from the alien attacks on people in the cars. Fortunately, she and Joe did not encounter any piles of human remains on the sidewalks and roadsides. When they approached the lake, they noticed the barricades that encircled it. Army trucks, fire engines and ambulances stood quietly at the ready, while various men and women in uniforms swarmed over the area. Some workers sifted through piles of remains, perhaps searching for identifying jewelry or insignia. Other individuals were scooping remains and placing them into plastic bags. There were no bystanders this time.

Andie edged as close to the sidewalk in the park as possible. She didn't want to cause trouble for the law enforcement officers, but she needed to see the spaceship. She and Joe stood staring at the black alien ship sitting in the lake. Andie had so many questions running rampant through her mind. She knew that this was the biggest thing that would ever happen to her, and probably, to every other human being as well.

# *CHAPTER 7*

"I'd rather have a sword coming out of the lake," said Joe.

"You and me and everyone else," muttered Andie. "Hey, do you think that the spaceship is a bit smaller than it was the first night?"

"I really can't tell," Joe admitted.

"Mm-hmm," Andie replied. She had a gut feeling that the spaceship had changed, but of course it was daylight now and the last time she'd seen the ship was at night.

"The newscasters said that maybe those smaller flying discs came from the body of these spaceships," she said.

"Like clones, or nanotechnology?"

"Yes, I guess. Because the small objects seem to be made of the same material as the larger spaceships. I guess we'll find out eventually."

"Or not," Joe said.

"Or not," Andie agreed. "I wonder what the aliens look like. Or maybe the small discs and the saucer in the lake are operated by remote control."

"It could be mind control, which sounds like something out of a *Star Trek* episode."

Andie surveyed the lake area then sighed.

"I don't see him," she said.

"Who?" asked Joe.

"Just this officer. I met him the other night. He brought me over here while everyone was going nuts trying to get away. His name is Frank Terranova. He seemed really nice."

"Oh. I hope he's okay. We can't really get close enough to talk to anyone." Joe's eyes swept the grounds of the small park.

"I know," Andie said as she continued to scrutinize the faces of emergency personnel a short distance away. "Wait! I think that's him coming down the path. Over there to the right."

She watched as the officer got closer and then enthusiastically waved. "Frank! Officer Frank! Over here!" The officer looked over with a squint. He raised his hand in greeting once he realized it was Andie making the commotion. Andie hadn't realized how tall Frank was until she saw him striding towards her. "There be giants," she murmured.

"What?" Joe asked.

"Oh, nothing." Andie pretended she hadn't said anything, but a blush travelled up her neck and into her cheeks. "Here he comes."

"Alrighty then," said Joe, amused by her reaction to the officer. "Listen, I'm going to head up to the shopping center to see if anything is open. How about I meet you back here in about a half hour?"

"Sure. Sure," she said. She briefly nodded to Joe then turned back to greet the officer. "Frank!" she called.

"Officer Terranova to you, young lady," Frank said as he approached. "You demonstrate a severe lack of respect for my badge."

Andie laughed. "Is that so? Should I salute you?" She gave a crisp salute. "Andie Thompson, reporting for duty, sir."

The officer stood several feet away on the other side of the barrier. He pulled aside some police tape and said, "Come on. I could use some company. Let's stow your bike in the bushes. No one is supposed to be over here except authorized individuals."

"What will we be doing? And by the way, I'm really glad to see you alive. So many..." She gestured towards the stakes that marked where people, officers and civilians alike, had taken their final breaths.

"Yeah. It was pure dumb luck. I was in my police car, and I just froze when I saw the alien discs come into the area. I lost some buddies in that attack. I still can't believe it." He shook his head, confusion and grief etched on his face.

"I'm so sorry," Andie said as she slipped under the police tape. She patted the officer's arm and blinked back tears.

He drew in a deep breath and lifted his head. "Anyway, I'm on surveillance detail with some other guys. We walk the path around the lake to make sure people are staying away."

"I can really come with you? You won't get into trouble?"

"Naw. They trust me, and anyway, it's hard to find officers who will take on this duty. Most of them went home to their families. Probably decided to go somewhere safer."

They started walking along the paved path, soon passing the dock and the place where Andie saw the frog flayed alive in the water. She shivered but said nothing.

"Who was the guy I saw you standing with, at the edge of the barrier?"

"Oh, that's Joe. He lives in my complex. We had our own brush with one of those discs the other day. It kind of bonds you to somebody when you experience terror together."

"That it does." They walked to the small bridge that overlooked the swampy back part of the lake and looked down into the brackish water. Usually, turtles could be seen sunning on rocks, but not today. They leaned on the railing and scanned the lake.

"Are we bonding, Officer Terranova?" Andie asked.

The officer guffawed then turned to Andie. "First, call me Frank. And second, tell me what you mean by bonding."

"Um, well, I guess I mean the type of bonding where we become good friends and share experiences together. Like this walk around the lake." She blushed again and even stuttered once.

"Mm-hm. Good friends and experiences. I might be able to do that." He stroked his chin as if thinking her offer over.

Andie nudged his side with her elbow. "You're pulling my leg."

Frank smiled, and said, "And now I'm pulling your arm because we have to keep moving." He tugged on her arm, and they both left the bridge and continued on the pathway. The surrounding trees had young green leaves with daffodils scattered around on the ground below.

"Where do you live, Frank? Close by?"

"Yes, over in Windham Woods. I have a nice townhouse. I live alone so there's plenty of space."

Andie noted the 'living alone' information and stored it away to mull over later.

"It's getting so pricey around here," Andie said. "I can barely afford a two-bedroom apartment on my teacher's salary." She looked up into the thinning woods at the town houses nestled above the lake. "Now those must go for a pretty penny." Frank followed her gaze, and nodded.

"Well, they used to be expensive. But now they're worth nothing. Everyone had to be evacuated from those homes, and heaven knows when they'll be able to return, if ever."

Andie almost stumbled but caught herself before she could fall.

"Easy, there. I don't want an injury on my watch."

"Sorry. I just realized the scope of this whole thing, and it shook me up a bit. Imagine having to give up your dream home. Forever?"

"Who knows? Maybe forever. The spaceships don't seem to be going anywhere. Speaking of which, the spaceship is just around the next corner. Are you up to seeing it close? It's only a few feet from the path."

"Okay. Yes, I really do want to see it."

The spaceship came into view within seconds. Andie's breath hitched as she took in the smooth perfection of the alien vessel. "It's so black, like outer space with no stars."

They stood staring for several minutes. The sheer alien nature of the celestial device had Andie in its thrall. "I wish I could touch it," she said.

"I wouldn't recommend it. Who knows what contaminants it has on its hull. And, remember the frog," Frank said.

Andie made a move to step closer to the ship when something in the spaceship changed. A panel high above their heads appeared and whipped open, revealing two red glowing orbs side by side.

"Don't move," Frank warned as the orbs stared at them. Just as suddenly as it appeared, the panel slid back over the opening and the orbs were gone. There were no seams in the ship's hull to indicate where the opening had been.

"Frack this," Andie yelled and ran as fast as she could away from the spaceship.

"Andie, wait!" Frank called, but Andie had no inclination to stop. Her feet were pounding the ground as her breath came in short gasps. She ran over the pathway by the dam and headed toward the parking lot. She saw Joe standing behind the police barrier and continued towards him. Just as she reached the tape, Frank grabbed her from behind.

"Andie, stop." Frank held on to her tightly as she kicked her legs and flailed her arms. "Andie, we're safe. It's not after us."

Andie stood still, then slid out of Frank's arms. She saw Joe watching them, open-mouthed with surprise.

"You okay now?" Frank asked, sweat pouring down his face from their frantic run.

"No. No one is okay. You saw those eyes."

Frank moved forward to hug Andie, and this time she let him hold her without fighting him.

"I'm not sure those were eyes, but Andie, I have to go and report this. It's our first sighting of

…whatever that was." Frank released Andie, and turned to Joe. "Take care of her. She just had a scare, and I think she needs something to counteract the shock."

Joe said, "No problem. I know just the place. Come on, Andie. "

Andie watched as Frank jogged across the field to a group of fellow officers. She nodded, and then looked at Joe. "You're not going to believe this."

# *CHAPTER 8*

Joe turned to her and said, "I checked out the shopping center up on Broken Land Parkway. It's only a little out of our way. You'll never guess what's open." He managed to pull her attention away from the lakeside.

"Really? Some places are still open for business? I heard on the news that looters are starting to hit the closed places," said Andie.

"We'll be careful. If we see anything unusual, we'll hightail it out of there," Joe promised. "Where's your bike?"

"Over in the bushes. Let me get it." With her heart beating faster than she could ever remember, she retrieved her bike and wheeled it under the police tape and over to Joe.

They climbed on their bikes and headed towards the shopping center. A few cars were still travelling on the roads, but the crashed cars were a large impediment to getting anywhere fast. The gas station at the front of the shopping center was open, and one car owner was pumping gas.

"That's good," said Andie. "I think I'll drive my car over and fill it up."

"Planning on going somewhere?" Joe asked.

"Probably," said Andie. Joe turned his head to look at her and saw her clenched jaw. He turned back to survey the shopping center and shouted in excitement, "Look! Dunkin is open! Woo-hoo!"

Andie laughed despite her state of shock. Sure enough, the Dunkin Donuts store looked open with its interior lights on. They wheeled up to the door and hopped off their bikes. Racing inside, they bumped into each other, vying to get to the counter first.

A Pakistani man with his Dunkin apron and white hat stood behind the cash register. "How may I help you?"

Andie stared at the array of donuts on the shelves before her. "This feels so unreal. Let's get a dozen assorted, Joe," she suggested.

"Yes! And two large coffees. I'll take mine black."

"Believe me, I don't need any caffeine. I'll take a lemonade," Andie added.

When their order had been filled and they had paid, they thanked the worker profusely and sat at a table near the windows at the front of the store. Andie crammed her mouth full of a strawberry- iced soft donut.

"Oh my god! Why do these donuts taste so good?" She shoved the last of the donut in her mouth and reached for a vanilla crème-filled one.

Joe watched Andie; he was glad she had lost the panicked look she'd had down at the lake, but the donut binging was disconcerting. "Whoa. Slow down, cowboy. You'll go into sugar shock if you aren't careful." He took a huge bite out of a cruller. "But you're right, these taste damn good." He wiped his mouth with a paper napkin. "So what happened at the lake, Andie?"

Andie brushed her hands of the donut crumbs and took a long sip of her lemonade through the straw.

"I saw an alien," she said.

Joe's eyes widened. "No shit? You saw one of the aliens? What did it look like?"

"I only saw the eyes. There was this sort of window that opened above me when I was standing right next to the spaceship. I saw two bright red eyes. I swear I thought it was going to pulverize me. But I stood still, and a few seconds later the window closed. Maybe it was an aperture, not a window. I don't know."

Joe sat back in his chair and whistled long and low. "Wow. That's scary."

"Beyond scary. It was…terrifying." She considered the remaining donuts but decided against eating another one.

"So there are beings in the spaceships. But are they humanoid or mechanical?"

"That remains to be seen. I'm curious, but I'm definitely not going back to the lake." She sighed heavily and said, "Let's head back home." They stood and placed their trash in the receptacle.

"I wonder how long he'll be able to stay open?" Andie inclined her head towards the worker behind the counter.

"Not too much longer, I'd think," Joe said. "Did you hear about the weird stuff out by Alpha Centauri?"

"Yeah," said Andie. "As Ray Bradbury said, something wicked this way comes." She stood by their table, fidgeting with the lid of the donut box.

"You know, I was wondering why the flying objects only come out at night? Why not during the daytime, too?"

"I was thinking about that. Maybe the bright light affects them somehow."

"It's weird to be able to move around in day light but have to be locked in at night. Of course, maybe they won't come at night again." Joe pondered for a moment, then his eyes opened. "I know this sounds crazy, but what if they are herding us? If they keep us indoors at night then we'll be easier to hunt and find when their masters come."

"Holy crap. That's really insidious." Andie slapped her hand down on the table. "That's it. I'm out of here."

The counter person whipped around at Andie's noise.

"Sorry. Sorry," she offered to the man. "I didn't mean this restaurant, although we will be leaving it soon. The donuts were great, but..." She noticed that the counter man had already turned away from her.

"I was thinking of leaving Columbia," Andie finished her sentence. They both sat back down at the table.

"I want to head up to the mountains," Joe stated.

"Me, too," Andie said. "I have a feeling it's not going to be safe here for too much longer. Well, it's not safe now, but you get what I mean."

"Where were you thinking of going?" he asked.

"Up to Acadia in Maine or down to the Shenandoah Valley in the Blue Ridge Mountains. I need to research it a bit and figure out what might work best." Andie peered into the donut box. Eight donuts remaining. "I have a brother up in Massachusetts, and he knows the mountains up there well. He and his wife hike on the weekends in the White Mountains in New Hampshire. I've actually climbed Mount Monadnock."

Joe clasped both hands down on the table. "Would you consider travelling together? You, me, and Satchmo?"

"Maybe I would," said Andie. "Where's your family located?"

"I just had my mom here in Baltimore, until she passed last year with cancer."

"Gosh, I'm sorry. That's rough. And your dad?"

"Never knew him," Joe added.

"I see," Andie said. "Well, let's do our research and think things over tonight." She was somewhat anxious at the thought of trusting a relative stranger.

"Sounds fair," Joe said. He peeked inside the donut box. "Let's split the leftovers. I'll get two bags from the guy." Joe stood up and went over to the counter.

Andie watched him carefully. It seemed that Joe considered her to be a capable partner for his escape from Columbia. She had a feeling that he was basically a good person. Heaven knows, he'd been through a lot in his young life with no family or parents. She thought that their partnership might lead them to a place of safety. Maybe they could find others that were also looking for a way to escape the aliens without fear of death. She thought of the red eyes that shone like an evil beast from hell. "Lord have mercy," she whispered.

# CHAPTER 9

Andie returned to her apartment building. After placing the bicycle back behind the bushes where she'd found it, she knocked again on Miss Bey's door. Within seconds, the door flung open and Miss Bey stood before her with a big smile and her be-wigged hair combed and curled.

"Why, Miss Bey," Andie said, "Aren't you a lovely sight for sore eyes!"

"Andie, if you got it, then you flaunt it, am I right?" Miss Bey's eyes twinkled. "I even got my good stockings on under this dress." She lifted her hem to show off her stockings to Andie.

Andie shook her head and laughed. Miss Bey was old school and a lady to the core, but she could be as cheeky as a teenager when the mood struck her. "Now Miss Bey, what are you doing all dressed up and nowhere to go? It's getting close to curfew, and no one is going out if those nasty little space things come flying around again."

"I dress to please myself, and no one else, and that's the truth." She sucked on her dentures.

"And that's why I like you, Miss Bey. You hold to your own rules. You don't let others tell you what to do." Andie reached out and laid her hand on the older woman's fragile arm.

"Listen, Miss Bey. I want to ask you something," Andie said.

"Well, ask away, baby. Ain't nobody stopping you."

"Miss Bey, I'm thinking of leaving tomorrow. I don't feel safe here anymore, and I want to put a lot of distance between me and any spaceship. Would you consider coming with me and my friend Joe? We're thinking of heading to the mountains." Andie cocked her head to the side and tried to read Miss Bey's thoughts. Miss Bey was silent for several moments then she placed her wrinkled hand over Andie's.

"Sweetie," she said. "That is truly kind of you to include me in your plans. But I assure you," she chuckled, "you don't want no old lady tagging along on your trip."

"Miss Bey, you wouldn't be an imposition at all, and there's plenty of room in my car." Andie removed her hand from Miss Bey's. "You see, I'm starting to get worried about that space anomaly that seems to be headed towards Earth." She wouldn't mention the alien eyes.

"Uh-huh," Miss Bey said. "That is a concern. I did listen to the news, and it seems that we might be in for more space stuff. I personally am not bothered by it. I have my sister, Louise, that I can talk to with that Skype, and as long as I can get down to the grocery store every now and then, I think I'll be all right."

Andie closed her eyes for a moment to collect her thoughts. "Miss Bey, I don't think the grocery stores or any other stores are going to be open too much longer. Those little killing machines are one thing. We seem to be able to hide from them during the day, but what if the bigger guns are coming? And what if they want to get rid of all of us, no matter what time of day it is?"

Andie continued, "I care about you, Miss Bey. I just want to be able to help, if I can. Where does your sister live?"

"She's just down in Manassas. Not far, but I'm afraid of driving those highways. The older I get, the worse the traffic seems to get."

"Well, Miss Bey," said Andie, "I'm not sure if the highways are crowded with traffic, per se, but there might be a lot of crashed cars due to the flying things."

"Oh, sweetie. I know. That's why I think I'll just stick close to my home where I have all my conveniences." She reached out to give Andie a warm hug then she released her.

"Miss Bey, what if I drove you down to Manassas tomorrow morning? Would you go? It would be right on my way to the Shenandoah Valley where I was thinking of going anyway." Andie became convinced that this would be the best thing for Miss Bey. She could be with her sister, and they could look out for one another.

Andie added, "I'm also taking Joe from one of the front buildings, but I know he'd be glad for your company."

Miss Bey sighed. "I tell you what. I'll think about it. Then I'll let you know in the morning. How does that sound?"

Andie breathed a sigh of relief. "That would be great. Thanks, Miss Bey. Now please get inside before it gets too dark."

Andie waved Miss Bey into her apartment. Once inside her own living room, she pulled out her computer and searched for information for the various mountain ranges on the East Coast. It didn't take long to affirm her decision to head down to the Blue Ridge Mountains. She was sure that she had made the right choice for everyone, even Satchmo. It was obvious that Miss Bey would be more comfortable with a beloved sister. With a lighter heart, she grabbed her Bradbury book, the one she'd tossed aside in her bedroom just two days ago and retreated to the comfortable living room couch with a bag of miniature chocolate bars in her hand. She was able to distract herself with the book and even fell asleep intermittently throughout the night.

The morning news brought even more terrible stories of deaths in the dark. The government was focusing its attention on developing a weapon to destroy the killing machines. Suppositions on whether the objects were related to the unknown mass headed towards Earth were presented. The capture of one of the small flying machines would help them to learn about how they worked, but this had yet to be achieved. When a grainy photograph of the large outer space mass was shown, even Andie could see that it was huge and would dwarf any human town or city.

She showered, dressed and walked to her garage that was a few buildings down from her own apartment. She opened her garage door and drove her Rav 4 to a parking spot in front of her building. Chewing bites of a bagel as she worked, Andie began to take armloads of boxes and packed bags to the car. She'd folded down one of the back seats to give more room for supplies but kept the other seat free in case Miss Bey decided to join her. After carefully placing all the foods and goods into the trunk, she covered the supplies with her tarp and piles of blankets and pillows. She squeezed in a suitcase full of clothing, including sweaters and jeans for cool evenings in the mountains. Just as she carried out her last load, which included a handful of photos of her friends and family members and her copy of *Dandelion Wine* as well as several other science fiction books, she noticed a police car driving through the apartment community. As the car came closer, Andie saw Officer Frank behind the wheel. She waved and walked over to him. "Hi! How are you doing? Not on lake duty anymore?"

The officer's window was rolled down due to the warm spring weather, and he called to her as he pulled up behind her car. "Hi, Andie. No, since our alien sighting, the lake is closed off to everyone, including the police."

Andie leaned on the car's door. "To be truthful, I'm glad to hear that. I was totally freaked out by seeing that thing. I was worried about you. Who knows what could happen?"

Frank reached out and patted her arm. "I appreciate your concern. I'll be as alert and careful as I can be. We don't need to lose any more cops."

"I am so sorry, Frank," Andie said as she remembered the loss of his friends.

"As I said, I was lucky. I just acted like a statue until the discs cleared out of the lake area. Of course, that saved my life."

"There were more than one of those flying things?" Andie asked.

"As far as we can tell, there were about a dozen flying around Columbia and some of the neighboring towns."

Andie took a deep breath. "My God. Well, at least they seem to come out only at night. It gives us a chance to do things." She pointed to the trunk of her car. "Like pack."

"I see," Frank said. "And where might you be headed?"

"Going south," replied Andie. "I thought the mountains might buy us some time and maybe some safety." She shrugged as if she wasn't totally convinced of her plan.

"Us? Who are you going with?" Frank ran his hand through his dark hair, then leaned closer to Andie.

"There's that guy I met who lives here in the complex. Joe. And he has a bulldog, Satchmo. I'm also taking an elderly woman, Miss Bey, to her sister in Virginia on the way to the Blue Ridge."

"Wow." Frank raised his thick eyebrows. "You have your hands full. But I could tell you were a get-it-done kind of gal from the other night when you faced that huge angry guy and stole his car," said Frank.

"For the record, I didn't steal his car. I just borrowed it for a minute. As I recall, it helped get you out of the traffic jam so you could get down to the lake!" Andie rolled her eyes at Frank.

"Oh, I'm not complaining, or accusing you in a court of law. I'm actually trying to give you a compliment. Strong women make the world go 'round." Frank might have been teasing at first, but he followed it up with such sincerity in his voice and dark eyes that Andie's heart melted.

Andie blushed, and shook her head. "Are you flirting with me, officer?"

Frank laughed out loud. "I might be. Or maybe it's bonding?"

"Yes," Andie agreed. "I like bonding. I feel comfortable with bonding. So, are you staying here, Frank? Do you have…um…people or family here?"

Andie's awkward question made her face feel hot again.

"Nope. No family, just some friends. No significant other." Frank winked as he revealed his personal status. "I want to stay and help out the department however I can, now that we are down so many men."

"That's noble, and as a citizen of this county, I thank you. I imagine there were some officers that were pressured to leave by their families," Andie said.

"Some. But not as many as you might think. We're a dedicated crew."

Andie smiled, and reached to rub Frank's shoulder through the window. "Take care, Frank. It's crazy out there."

"You, too, Andie. Maybe we'll see each other again when this is all over." He reached up and placed his hand over Andie's. There was a moment of silence between them that was charged with an underlying tension.

Andie leaned into the car and kissed Frank on his cheek. She then stepped away from the police car. "Bye, Frank," she whispered.

"Goodbye, pretty lady," Frank said as he turned the wheel and pulled away.

Miss Bey's door banged open, and Miss Bey slowly came outside, weighed down with two large flowered tote bags and wearing a straw wide-brimmed hat.

"I'm coming!" Miss Bey called. "I called my sister and told her to expect me today. She was happier than a rabbit sucking down fresh pansies."

Andie laughed and reached to take Miss Bey's bags. "I'm so glad! I feel much better knowing that you'll be somewhere safe with your sister. Take the back seat and spread out your things on top my stuff." She looked up and saw Joe and Satchmo walking towards them. "Here come the others."

She reached down to scratch Satchmo's head as he plopped at her feet.

"Hi, guys," Andie said. Joe replied with a smirk. "He already likes you."

"He has good taste," Andie quipped. "Looks like we're off to the mountains. Miss Bey is coming with us, but only as far as Manassas. I'm dropping her off at her sister's." Joe waved to Miss Bey, who was fussing with her bags in the back seat.

"That's cool. I guess I can figure out where we're going-the Blue Ridge, right?"

"Bingo. It's the closest. I can get there pretty easily. And the weather is more comfortable going south at this time of year. There's lots of cabins and places to bunk in. Skyline Drive will be the first place we can go but we can easily head down to North Carolina if we need to."

"And we can drop off Miss Bey along the way," Joe added.

Andie laughed, "Yeah. And that, too. She's kind of special to me."

"Like I said, it's totally cool. I had come to the same decision about the Appalachian Mountains last night. I'm just hoping everyone else hasn't decided to head to those hills with us," Joe said.

"The mountains are big enough to hide a lot of people. For now," Andie commented.

Joe nodded. "Can you take Satch and me back to my apartment? Everything is packed and ready to go." He picked up Satchmo and placed him in the foot well of the front passenger's seat, and then he slipped into the seat without putting on the seatbelt.

The bonging of the seatbelt alarm made Andie roll her eyes. "Like to live dangerously, huh?" she teased Joe.

"Not really," he replied. "But sometimes circumstances make it necessary."

Miss Bey chimed from the back seat in hearty agreement. "That they do, darlin'. That they do."

# *CHAPTER 10*

Once Joe had run up to his apartment and gathered his gear, he stashed it all into the jammed trunk of the Rav 4. He joined the others inside the car, this time fastening his seat belt.

Andie stopped at the gas station they'd seen yesterday and topped off her gas tank. Joe noted that the Dunkin' Donuts was closed up tight.

"No more glazed donuts," he mourned.

"No more strawberry frosted," Andie chimed in.

"No more nothing," Miss Bey muttered. "Those dang nasty aliens done took away all the good stuff." All of the shops in the center were closed for business with no signs of any activity or people.

"Hang in there, Miss Bey," Andie said. "Maybe some stores will still be open in Virginia."

"Be that as it may, I'm leaving behind my gorgeous mahogany breakfront, and I don't feel none to happy about it." Miss Bey stared out the window as Andie drove towards the highway entrance.

"You can come back and get it when this is all over," said Joe.

"That's true, young man. No one can lift that thing by himself. It took 6 men to move it into that apartment. It's going to stay right where it is." Miss Bey let a smile slip from the corner of her mouth. "Hoo-ee! I'd like to see someone try."

The drive going south on Interstate 95 was fairly hazardous, with many cars piled up on the sides and some newer crashes and stoppages to weave around. None of the cars had people inside, and Andie didn't wish to mention it with Miss Bey in the car. There could be piles of ash and bones on the car seats. They noticed some cars moving in either direction, but traffic was light. Sometimes children waved from the back seats, and Miss Bey was sure to return their greetings. Somewhere around Washington, D. C., Miss Bey could be heard snoring in the back seat. Andie looked at Joe, and they both shared a smile. Joe pointed down at his feet, and sure enough, Satchmo had also fallen into a deep slumber.

"Let me know if you want me to take over the driving," Joe said.

"I'm good for now. I have adrenaline running through my veins instead of blood. I could push this car down the highway with my arms if I had to."

Joe nodded. "I know what you mean. Now that we've decided to leave Maryland, I just want to be in the mountains."

"Is this for real? Are we running to escape aliens? What the hell happened to my normal life?" Andie asked.

"It disappeared the day those spaceships landed. Believe me, I'd love to be at work, processing claims and drinking black coffee by the bucket load."

"Where do you work?" Andie asked.

"Eh, I was at a small company down in Virginia that contracted with the government. I was just a cog in the machine. A successful cog, but a cog nevertheless."

"A lot of my friends have similar jobs. God, I hope everyone's okay. It's like everyone just disappeared. I suppose they went to be with family. With the spotty cell phone service, I couldn't reach anyone." She thought about her brother and his wife. If only she could have gotten in contact with him. They were so much alike, with the same values, sense of humor, and love of the ocean.

Joe interrupted her thoughts. "Yeah. It was a crap shoot. I got to talk to one of my buddies for a few minutes. He and his wife were heading out to Pennsylvania. There's a lot of good countryside there, so I'm sure he'll do alright. He's a smart guy."

Andie began to feel guilty. "I should have tried my phone more. I was just in such shock. I could only think about staying alive. That seems so selfish now…"

"Not at all. Every living thing is trying to make it from day to day. We don't have any experience with something like this. Heck, like you said, it's aliens." Joe closed his eyes and rubbed his brow and eyelids.

When he opened his eyes, Joe flung out an arm and pointed down the highway. "Stop the car! Pull over! It's one of those damn flying things!"

Andie swerved over to the fire lane of the highway and turned off the car. "Are you sure?" she whispered.

"Don't move. Don't even talk," Joe hissed.

The small black flying object came soaring at them at whiplash speed. In the back seat, Miss Bey was asleep and unaware of the danger just outside the windows. Andie held herself still and closed her eyes. She was aware of Joe beside her, frozen in his seat.

They could hear the object come up to the front windshield then make a slow circle around the car. Andie felt her heart beating in her throat.

The object veered to the bushes alongside the road, perhaps sensing the movement of a small animal or bird. "Don't move," Joe said again.

From the back seat, Miss Bey called, "Hey, why we done stopped? Did we run out of gas?"

Andie and Joe could see Miss Bey sitting up and stretching from her brief nap. "Miss Bey, there's a flying object in the bushes. Stay still," Andie cautioned.

Miss Bey turned her head to the side, searching for the space object. "Oh, those nuisances. I have had enough of them! They need to go back where they came from." As she finished her tirade with an arm sweep up to the ceiling of the car, the black object emerged from the green bush and headed straight for the car. Within seconds, the killing device shot its laser straight at

Miss Bey and penetrated the car window. Miss Bey was gone. A pile of matter on the car seat was the only indication that she'd been there just moments before. A small hole in the window beside Miss Bey was the only damage that had been done to the car. There was no smoke and no residual heat from the laser.

"Noooo!" screamed Andie. Satchmo barked from the floor right under Joe's feet.

"Don't move, Andie. Satchmo, hush!" Joe said through the side of his mouth, barely moving his lips.

The small spacecraft completed another circle around the car. It then continued down the highway, going north.

"Stay still. Just for another minute. Until it gets out of sight," Joe said.

Andie began shaking, tears leaking from the corners of her eyes. "Miss Bey…" she called gently. "Not Miss Bey, no, no, no…"

Joe moved his hand to cover hers on the wheel of the car. "Andie, you have to hold it together. We have to get to safety."

Andie dropped her hands to her lap. "It's my fault. It's all my fault. I convinced her to come, Joe! She wanted to stay in Columbia. But I said I'd take her to Virginia. I made her die!" Andie's voice began to rise, and she was yelling by the end of her words. "I killed Miss Bey!"

Joe grabbed her wrists and turned Andie to face him. "Stop it, Andie. You didn't kill Miss Bey. No one did. Maybe she didn't realize that the object could get her in the car. She drew its attention when she began shaking her arm at it. You have to pull yourself together or you'll be the next one to get cremated."

Andie took a deep sobbing breath. "Why did she do that? It's like she was taunting the object."

"Maybe she'd had enough. She might have realized that she wouldn't really be safe down in Virginia with her sister. Maybe she thought she'd be a burden to her sister."

"Then why did she come?" Andie moaned.

"She wanted to please you. She cared for you as much as you cared for her. I think we need to stop thinking about why it happened. It could drive us crazy and nothing can come out of it."

"What are we going to do with her remains?" Andie's voice shook.

"When we get away from these populated areas, I'll gather her ashes into a bag. We can bury her in the mountains," Joe said.

"I'll look to see if her sister's address is in one of her bags, but it seems like the bags are filled with clothing."

"Good idea. Let's do that now, then we can continue the trip. I'll drive the next leg." Joe kept an eye out for space discs while Andie reached back and grabbed Miss Bey's bags. As suspected, there was no identifying information for Miss Bey's sister.

"Okay, do you mind changing places?" Joe asked. "We'll have to do it and pray that no more objects swing by. You'll also have to sit with Satchmo for now. Later we can rig something for him in the back seat if we need to."

"Okay," Andie responded. "Let's do it."

The changeover was swift and successful. Andie reached down to pet Satchmo. "You're a good boy, such a good boy," she murmured. Joe started the car and carefully pulled back out on to the highway.

"I'm going to drive slower. Now that the objects are out in the daytime, or at least this one is, I'll need to be able to control the car at a moment's notice." He looked over at Andie. Her face was pale, and her eyes were focused ahead.

"You handled that pullover like a champion, Andie."

Andie gave a weak smile then settled her head back against the head rest with her eyes closed. "Yeah," she said. "Too bad Miss Bey had to die."

# CHAPTER 11

Andie became the point man, searching ahead and behind for rogue space discs. It was a tiresome job, with her neck becoming sore from all the slow and careful movements. Joe drove cautiously, always aware that he might need to stop at a moment's notice.

As they travelled through northern Virginia, outside of the business corridor and beyond Dulles airport, they both spotted a stopped car ahead. A family of five stood outside their Caravan, a mother, father, two boys about ten or eleven years old and a small girl. They were waving and calling, attempting to flag down Andie's car.

"Joe, stop! Those people!" Andie shouted out in warning.

But Joe continued driving by the clustered family, who stood shocked with their mouths wide open in mute surprise.

Andie turned around and looked backwards at the stranded family. They stood stock still, watching the Rav 4 recede from them, yard by hopeless yard.

"What the hell are you doing?!" Andie blasted Joe. "We need to save those people. They're sitting ducks out there on the highway." She turned to stare at Joe.

Joe's mouth was closed, his lips clamped in a tight line.

"Stop this car, right now!" Andie yelled at him.

Joe shook his head in a tight negative movement. "We can't, Andie. We don't have enough room."

"Who are you, some monster?" Andie squeezed the words out.

"I'm doing the right thing. For us, Andie. For you, me and Satch," Joe said. "We have to think about our supplies. With five extra people, even if we could fit them in this car, we'd be out of food in a week, or less."

"That's selfish and inhumane," Andie said.

"Andie, do you really want to play Sophie's Choice? Because that's what would have happened if we had stopped for that family. They would have seen that there was no room for all of them, and they would have divided the family up. They would have given us the mom and the little girl, and the father and boys would have been left behind."

"Shouldn't that choice have been left up to them? Who do you think you are, a God?"

"No, I'm just a scared man who is hoping that another van or truck comes by who can take the whole family to safety before a black space machine comes and kills them all." Joe banged the steering wheel with his fist. "Dammit, Andie, I'm doing the best I can." He began to sob, with tears cascading down his cheeks.

Andie's heart stopped as she watched her companion fall to pieces, much as she had done after Miss Bey had died. She nodded to herself and turned back to watching the road ahead.

"Okay. I'm sorry," she whispered.

"Things have changed. The world has changed. It's hard to know what's right or wrong," Joe said.

"Yes."

They travelled without speaking for the next half hour, until they reached Front Royal and the northern entrance to Shenandoah National Park and Skyline Drive. The gatehouse was empty, with no toll keeper to collect the usual fees. Joe pulled the car over to the side of the road under some hanging tree branches.

"Satchmo needs a break," Joe announced. The area looked deserted, with no other cars in sight, so Andie opened her car door and helped to let Satchmo out of the foot well. Satch lumbered over to some stone outcroppings to do his business. Joe and Andie stared off into the distance of the state park. The spring trees were tipped with light green, and wildflowers edged the road.

"I thought we could check out the lodging here in the park. There are two main places along Skyline Drive that have rooms or cabins to rent. I figure it's worth a shot," Andie said.

Joe glanced at Andie. "Sure," he said. Then turned his attention to Satchmo.

"Do you mind keeping an eye on Satch?" he asked. "I thought I'd clean, I mean take care of, the back seat."

Andie remembered Miss Bey's remains with a start, and said, "Oh! I have a clean plastic bag. Just give me a minute to find the box. It's in the back with all my other stuff. I thought the bags might be useful." Her patter soon died into silence as she searched the rear of the car.

"Here," she said as she handed over the bag to Joe. "And . . . thanks." Andie walked over to Satchmo, took hold of his leash and began to stroll away from the car. She couldn't, and she wouldn't, watch Joe's ministrations. The pain burned like fired iron against her heart. Satchmo, oblivious to the emotions churning within Andie, nosed his way through dirt and stones in the warm spring air.

"All set," Joe called, and Andie walked back to the car. "I put the bag in the back so that we can scatter her ashes or bury them somewhere nice. Is that okay with you?" Joe said in a gentle voice that almost caused her to break down again.

"That's fine, Joe. I appreciate what you've done," Andie said.

"Okay, then. Let's get to that lodge. How far do you think it is from here?"

Andie thought a moment. "Skyland is about 40 miles, give or take a few. It's at the highest point along the drive, too. If I remember correctly, it's a pretty big place. Then there's another resort further down Skyline called Big Meadows Lodge. But Skyland is our best bet."

"So, you've been here before?" Joe asked.

"A long time ago, when I was a kid. And the internet had some good information on it when I checked last night," Andie said.

"I don't know what to expect when we get there. Either the place will be packed, or it could be empty."

"As long as it's safe," Andie added.

"It seems pretty clear up here," Joe said. "This was a good idea, coming up to the mountains."

"I hope so. The original mountain people loved it until they were kicked out in the 1930's. It's sad that everyone who used to live here was relocated outside of the park just so that we all could enjoy the mountains and fresh air."

"It's like the resettlement of the Native Americans," Joe observed.

"Yes. Apparently, there are ruins of former homes and graveyards along Skyline Drive. The old roads were made into fire roads by the National Forestry, and you can still see them, if they aren't totally grown over by vegetation."

"I've been thinking about water supplies. We can get situated by a stream for fresh water."

"Or a spring," Andie noted.

"I brought a fishing rod with us," Joe said. "I've had one for ages and never used it. Columbia was supposed to have decent fishing."

"I think I recall seeing fishermen somewhere in Columbia, but I'm glad to hear we have a rod with us. It'll be nice to have fresh food to supplement our canned stuff."

They travelled along the Skyline Drive, marveling at the incredible mountain views as they negotiated the road's twists and turns. Several deer grazed in a field of fresh grass while birds soared overhead.

"We'll have to watch out for bear," Andie said. "They're pretty common around here."

"I also packed a gun," Joe said. Andie's head whipped around.

"What? Are you kidding me?"

"Nope. I have a pistol I inherited from an uncle." Joe shrugged. "I've never used it, and I hope I don't have to. But it feels good to have it along."

"I suppose," Andie said. "Black bear can get pretty big. I've seen them crossing the road when I traveled through the Laurel Mountains. Wouldn't want to mess with them."

"It's in my tackle box in the back. The gun, I mean. And it's loaded."

Andie laughed. "That reminds me of the time after my dad died and my mom found a gun in the night table next to his bed. There were also a couple of boxes of bullets. She was totally freaked out and asked me and my brother to get them out of the house immediately. We carried the gun and ammo to the police station as if they were delicate cakes with our arms extended in front of us. The cop who checked them out said the gun was loaded, and that we were lucky we hadn't shot our toes off."

"Guns are no joke. They can be dangerous if you don't know what to do with them," Joe said. "Remind me to teach you how to use it."

"Sure," Andie replied. "I don't want to lose my toes."

"I see your sense of humor is coming back."

"Yeah. Gallows humor." Andie watched the passing mountain tops and the deep blue valleys in silence for a few minutes. She was glad that her parents were no longer alive to experience the current horrors in the world. She thought of sweet Miss Bey and shuddered with the emotional pain of her grief. She had caused Miss Bey's death, and that was a fact she would have to live with for the rest of her life. She couldn't even remember Miss Bey's first name. She didn't even know if Miss Bey had ever been married. She closed her eyes for a while and at some point nodded off. She startled when she heard Joe calling out, "Hey, there it is! The first lodge that you told me about."

Andie peered down the highway. There it was, as she remembered it from her childhood trip along Skyline Drive, the Skyland Hotel. The simple structure, with wood and cement, backed into woods that bordered stunning vistas.

"Pull over. Let's stop and see if anyone's there."

Joe slowed the car down to a crawl as they approached the resort, then stopped a short distance away from the front of the main building. They could see a row of log cabins further in the woods. Andie rolled down her car windows. She could hear nothing except the chirping of birds in the trees, and the call of a hawk from above. Andie took a deep breath of the cool, clean air, and started to feel like herself again, if that was possible, under the circumstances.

# CHAPTER 12

"Where is everybody?" she whispered. "I don't see any people."

"Maybe they're inside." Joe gestured to the main building. "There are a bunch of cars in the parking lot down the road."

Andie nodded then said, "I don't want to park down the road. Do you think we could park right in front, closer to the building?"

Joe laughed. "I don't see why not. There are no rules, as far as I'm concerned. The aliens took care of that."

"Okay. Park the car, and we'll check this place out. If there aren't many campers, maybe we could stay in one of the cabins."

They exited the car with Satchmo in tow. When they got within a few feet of the door, Joe stopped and looked around. "I think I'll tie Satch up to this post. Not everyone likes dogs, and he'll be comfortable sleeping under the shade of these trees." Joe fastened Satchmo's leash, gave it a tug to check if it was secure then pet his dog on the head. "Stay here, boy. We'll be back soon."

Andie reached for the metal handle of the wood door and pulled it open with a strong tug. She and Joe entered into the quiet and cool lodge, looking around at the clean and comfortable surroundings.

"Hello?" Andie called out.

Suddenly, a door to their right pushed open as a large man in a plaid shirt and dark- colored jeans burst into the foyer. Andie let out a slight scream.

"Hey, hey. I'm sorry!" the man said. "I didn't mean to scare you folks."

Andie put a hand over her heart, willing the fast beat to slow. "Oh, but you did. Phew." Joe put his arm protectively around Andie's shoulders.

The man, with craggy facial features and penetrating blue eyes, opened and closed his fists. "I said I was sorry."

Joe jumped in saying, "Yes, you did. And that is appreciated. Right, honey?"

Andie gave Joe the side eye, wondering what he was up to. She was not his honey, so this must be some ruse.

"Uh, right. Honey. Thank you for the apology, sir." Andie stuttered her words.

The man took several seconds to reply, "Okay, then. What are you folks looking for?"

"Well," Joe's words were slow and measured, "I guess we were wondering if you were serving some food." He pointed to the dining room to the left. "We're kind of hungry, and we were hoping you were still in business."

"Why wouldn't we be?" the man asked.

Joe smiled, while his arm tightened around Andie's shoulders. "No reason; no reason at all. I mean, there's the stuff about the aliens, but that doesn't mean anything here, does it?"

The man's eyes narrowed. "No such thing as aliens."

"Oookay, so do you think we could have some burgers and fries? By the way, I'm Joe, and this is Andie."

The man unclenched his fists and extended his arm towards the dining room. "The name's Buck. Seat yourselves." He walked back through the swinging door.

Andie and Joe took the nearest table and slid into their wood chairs.

"What's with the honey thing?" Andie asked.

"I just have a bad feeling about that guy. We need to stick close together until we figure out what's going on."

They looked up as Buck entered the dining room and slapped down two glasses of water on the table. He left the room again.

"He doesn't believe in aliens," Andie said.

"Seeing is believing," Joe replied.

Andie looked around the large dining room, with the large oak tables and wood chairs. Floor to ceiling windows overlooked the forest, sunlight streaming through the branches. It would be a beautiful place, she thought, except…

"Where are the people?" she whispered.

"Good question," Joe said.

"I don't hear any burgers cooking in the kitchen," she commented.

"I think we should…" His words were covered by a fierce barking. Satchmo's barking.

Joe and Andie stood as one and then raced to the main door of the lodge. As they opened it, they saw Satchmo pulling at his leash, trying to run toward Andie's car. His barking was insistent, with teeth bared and his claws digging into the dirt. Andie looked up and saw two men opening the doors of her car. She gasped, and turned to Joe. At that moment, Satchmo managed to free himself from the post and run towards the men.

"No, Satch. Stop!" Joe yelled.

But Satchmo didn't stop until he was at the car and had Buck's leg in his snarling mouth. The other man backed off but then picked up a solid tree branch and began hitting Satchmo.

"Get back inside," Joe ordered Andie. He then ran towards the car. When he got close to the Rav 4, he bent over and crouched, working his way to the back of the vehicle.

Andie couldn't move. She gazed at the horrific scene of Satchmo mauling Buck's leg, and the other man attacking Satchmo. Then a third man came running from the woods. In his hands he carried a rifle. He pointed the rifle at Satchmo. "Get away!" he yelled to the men. The man with the tree branch moved a few feet away, but Buck had now fallen to the ground. The rifleman stopped and aimed his gun at Satchmo. A shot exploded through the air, and Satchmo fell down. Instantly, a second shot rang out, only this time the gunman fell to the ground, holding his leg at the knee.

Andie whipped her head around to see Joe at the back of the car, leaning against the window. Somehow, he had retrieved his own gun, and now he was a player in this nightmare. Joe got off another shot, and this time he grazed the head of the man beside Buck. The man screamed and ran towards the woods. Joe sidled towards Satchmo and Buck. Buck was groaning and trying to pull himself away to safety. Joe picked up a rigid Satchmo and placed him into the front seat of the car.

"Come on!" he called to Andie.

She ran to the car, slid into the backseat while Joe took over the front. Joe gunned the gas pedal, and the car screeched as Joe turned it towards the highway, one hand holding Satchmo in the front passenger seat.

"Shit!" Joe said. "They got Satch. They got him!"

"Where?" Andie cried. "Where did he get hit? Is he alive?"

"I can't tell." Joe was sweating, his voice frantic.

"Stop the car for a second and give him to me."

"We have to get out of here." Joe's voice raised a few notches towards panic.

"Just stop for a second. It's okay," Andie commanded.

Joe stopped the car, and got Satchmo out of his seat. He handed the dog to Andie.

"Now drive! Fast!" she ordered him.

Andie held Satchmo on her lap. Satchmo was actually awake and breathing but he was so quiet. She noticed blood on her pants and then saw that one of Satchmo's legs had a jagged tear. She grabbed one of Miss Bey's bags and found a scarf. She wrapped the scarf tightly around the dog's leg to staunch the blood flow. He would need his wound to be cleaned, and some antiseptics as well.

Andie breathed a loud sigh of relief. "He's okay, Joe. He's going to be fine. The bullet got his leg, but it's not too deep, I think. We need to get him somewhere so we can take care of him."

"Oh, God," Joe said as tears ran down his face. "Satchmo, buddy. I love you, big guy."

"He knows," Andie said as she pet the dog's back. "And he loves you right back."

# *CHAPTER 13*

The sun was falling lower in the sky as Joe frantically drove the Rav 4 down Skyline Drive. He pushed the speed limit where he could but the hairpin turns had to be negotiated or they would all be tossed over a guardrail into the rock canyon below. They passed the other hotel, the Big Meadows Lodge, without commenting. Their one mountain lodge experience for the day had made them cautious.

"What's the plan?" Andie asked from the backseat, as she held the quivering Satchmo.

"I think I remember from the map I saw online yesterday that there's a small town somewhere south of here. Twenty or thirty miles. Maybe they have a doctor or a vet."

"Yes, I remember seeing that, too. It's called Waynestown or Waynesboro, something like that."

"Right."

"It seems as if the aliens haven't made it up to these mountains, yet. I haven't seen any of the flying discs."

"No, no monsters up here except the human kind," Joe said.

"I wonder what those idiots have done with other people? We can't have been the first visitors up here." Andie ran her fingers through the fur on Satchmo's head.

"I don't want to think about it." Joe's voice was sharp and angry.

"You really saved the day with that gun of yours, Joe. I...don't know how to say thanks, except...thanks."

"It was Satch who saved us, Andie. He created the diversion so that I could get to the gun. Without Satchmo grabbing that guy's leg, I would never have made it. That dog saved my life." Tears kept rolling down Joe's cheeks. He swiped his arm across his face to clear his eyes. "Now we have to save him."

Andie spotted a sign on the side of the road that read, Waynesboro Five Miles. "Joe, this must be the exit for that town."

Joe slowed down the Rav 4 and took the exit ramp on to a small two-lane highway. Houses dotted the side of the road here and there, with an occasional small shop interspersed.

"I'm going to find the main area of town. We're likely to find more people there, if there are any," said Joe.

As the buildings multiplied and grew closer together, Joe drove slow enough so they could read the signs in store windows.

"Not much is open," Andie commented.

Joe pulled over to a small restaurant that had lights shining through the storefront windows. 'Eat at Ed's' flashed in blue neon.

"Any particular reason you stopped here?" Andie wondered.

"Yeah," Joe muttered as he unbuckled his seat belt. He pointed to the dark building next door, where a small sign in tailored script read 'H. Weinstein, Veterinarian.' Joe opened the back door and slid his arms to Andie so that she could place Satchmo in his grasp. "Come on, big guy," he whispered.

"I'll go ahead and see if I can find anyone," Andie said. She ran up to the vet's office and tried the door. Locked. She banged on the door and called out, "Hello! Anyone? We need help!" She banged again on the door, but no one answered.

Andie ran to the restaurant next door and opened the door just before Joe stepped in behind her, cradling Satchmo. The bells above the door rang, an irritating cacophony. A young woman, about thirty or so with her sandy hair pulled back in a tight pony tail, poked her head out from the kitchen in the back of the restaurant.

"Hey! What's with all the noise? And wait a second. No dogs allowed in here!" She walked over to Joe and placed her hands on her hips. "No dogs. It says it on the sign in the window. By order of the Department of Health."

Andie walked around Joe and touched the other woman's arm. "Can you please help us? Our dog has been shot by some insane men up on Skyline Drive. He needs a vet. Where can I find the vet?"

The woman looked down at Satchmo, and her eyes softened. "Oh my God, how bad is he hurt?"

"Real bad," Andie said.

"Well," the woman said, "I saw Dr. Weinstein leave about an hour ago. His apartment is above the office, so he shouldn't be out too long. There's isn't much to do around here these days. The town is clearing out because of, well, aliens."

"I guess we'll go and wait in the car for the doctor," Joe said, turning back towards the door. "Thanks, anyway."

"No, no. That's okay. Seriously, you can stay. It's warmer here, and maybe you can order a bite to eat while you wait." The woman rubbed her hands on her apron, then extended her hand to Andie. "I'm June Carver."

"I'm Andie, and this is Joe. He's holding Satchmo. We can't thank you enough for your hospitality. We've been through so much today."

"Take a booth. You can lay Satchmo down on the seat. In fact, I have some towels we could put under him." June ran to the kitchen and returned with a pile of clean white towels. She placed them neatly to make a comfortable rest area for Satchmo. "There. Done. That should work." She backed away as Joe laid Satchmo down. Satchmo whimpered, and Joe slipped into the seat next to him. "It's okay, boy," he said to comfort the dog, running his hand gently over Satchmo's head.

"I've had dogs, though I don't have any now. I know how much they can get under your skin and into your heart," June said. She looked down at Satch with concern and caring.

Joe looked up and smiled. "You can say that again. Listen, thanks for this. Like Andie said, it's been a real nightmare, and we are appreciative of your kindness."

"It's nothing," June blushed and smoothed down her apron again. "Now how about some coffee while you decide on something to eat? Here's two menus." She slipped the plastic-covered meal choices on to the table and walked away.

"From hell to heaven," said Andie, observing the warm-heartedness of the waitress and trying to forget the horror of their reception at Skyland.

June returned with two steaming coffees and took their orders of hamburgers and fries.

"I don't usually eat this much junk food. Oreos the other day, then donuts yesterday," Joe remarked.

"Yes, but when in Rome . . ."

"Or a greasy diner," Joe added. He sighed between sips of his coffee. "I just hope that Dr. Weinstein comes home soon and hasn't left town."

June sauntered over to their table. "I've put on the burgers and dunked the fries, so it'll be just a few minutes."

"June, have the aliens, you know, the small flying discs, been to this town?" asked Andie.

"God, no! And I pray they never will. We've all seen it on TV, and it is beyond believing." Her eyes were bright and round. "Lots of folks left town to be with their kinfolk, but me and Dan are staying put for the duration."

"Is Dan your husband?"

"Yeah, been married five years. Hope to be married fifty more." She started walking back to the kitchen. "But he's a trucker, and he's on a run. I don't expect him back for a few more days." June disappeared back into the kitchen.

Andie met Joe's eyes. They both knew the chances of survival on the open road were slim.

"Soo . . ." Andie said. She peered over the table at Satchmo, lying on his bed of towels. "We need to get this dog fixed. And I don't mean in the usual way."

Joe smiled wanly as June brought their loaded plates to the table. The juicy burgers and crispy fries were appealing since they hadn't eaten since the morning.

"Thanks, June," Andie called out.

"My pleasure," June said and left to wipe tables across the small room.

Satchmo lifted his head, as if to try and get closer to the food but his injuries stopped him. Joe winced and said, "Satch, after you get fixed up, I'm going to get you the biggest burger this town can make. That's a promise."

Satch made another whimpering noise then fell asleep to escape his pain.

When Andie and Joe were done with their satisfying meal, they sat back and took in their surroundings. "Who owns this place?" Joe asked June, calling to her from across the room.

"Oh, that would be Mr. Evans. He left town this morning and asked me to keep things running. But it's not like folks are lining up at the door to get in." June walked over to their table. "I figure I'll keep it open until no one shows up. Ed, I mean Mr. Evans, has been good to me. Plus, what the heck else am I going to do with Dan out of town?"

"June," Joe began tentatively. "I was wondering if you could recommend a place we could stay for the night. Once Satchmo is taken care of by the vet, he's going to need to rest for a while. We'd hoped to make camp somewhere up in the mountains, but that's going to have to wait."

"Well, let me see. The best hotel in this town is the Holiday Inn, but it's closed. Tourists don't usually get up this way so early in the year. And, of course, there's the extraterrestrials." She tapped her fingers on her lips. "Okay! You know what? You all can stay upstairs. There's a small apartment that Mr. Evans used sometimes when he'd stay late working on the books and such. It has a bed, a table and chairs. It's not a palace, or a hotel room, but it might work for you."

Andie's eyes filled with tears. "That is more than kind, June. In fact, it's perfect."

"Well, don't say that until you see it. Wait!" she exclaimed. "I think I just saw Dr. Weinstein's coat go by." June ran to the door and leaned out to call, "Dr. Weinstein! Come here, please! We need your help!"

June turned and faced Andie and Joe. "He's coming. Everything is going to be all right now."

# *CHAPTER 14*

A slim, grey-haired man entered the restaurant as June filled him in on Satchmo's injuries. "He's right over here, Doc."

Dr. Weinstein removed a cap, placed it on the nearest table and walked over to where Andie and Joe were seated. "So let me see this pup of yours," he said. Joe stood up so that the doctor could get a better look at Satchmo as he lay on the bench. Andie held her breath and prayed. The doctor moved Satchmo's legs and turned him to better examine his wounds.

"Let's get him next door, pronto," the doctor advised. "This guy needs surgery, not to mention antibiotics and pain meds."

Joe once again scooped up Satchmo and ran behind the doctor to his office. Andie stood up more slowly. She reached into her pocket and pulled out her wallet. "June, what do we owe you for dinner?"

"Give me a ten and we'll call it square," June said.

Andie knew the bill came to more that ten dollars, so she pressed a twenty into June's hands. "Keep the tip," she winked at June.

"Thanks," June said. "And listen, I'll keep the restaurant open until you get back. I hope Satchmo does okay. He's in good hands with Dr. Weinstein."

Andie waved a good-bye then walked over to the vet's office. This time the door opened freely, and Andie was able to walk in. The reception area was empty and dark, but a light down a hallway led to an examining room. The doctor was bent over Satchmo while Joe sat nervously twisting his hands in a nearby chair. He hopped up when he saw Andie. "Satch is under sedation now so the doc is cleaning the wounds."

Andie waved Joe into the hallway. "Let's go sit in the waiting room, and leave the doctor to his work." Joe nodded and followed Andie down the hall.

They sat side by side in scalloped plastic chairs, breathing in the smells of animals and pet food. "Do you think he has some other animals here tonight?" Andie asked.

"I don't know, but I don't think so. It's too quiet." Joe tapped his fingers on the chair arms. "Thanks for being here, Andie."

"A girl can eat only so many fries. And those pies under the glass domes were looking too tasty," Andie said.

"I hope he makes it," Joe whispered hoarsely.

"He will," Andie replied. "He's a tough old bird."

After an hour of tense waiting, Dr. Weinstein walked towards them. He pulled down his face mask and removed his plastic gloves. "Okay, then," he remarked.

Joe jumped up like a live wire. "Is he okay? Is he going to make it?"

The doctor nodded his head in recognition of Joe's worry. "I think so. I've cleaned out the wounds and sutured him. He's on a drip for fluids and meds. We'll be able to know better in the morning, but for now he's going to be sleeping. I'm keeping him here overnight. I have a comfortable cage that will keep him safe. Is that alright by you?"

Joe took a deep breath and answered, "Definitely. Whatever he needs."

Andie added, "We'll be staying next door in the apartment above the restaurant. Just call if you need us."

Joe handed the doctor a card with his cell phone number printed on it. The doctor placed the card on the counter of the reception desk. "Good night, then."

"Good-night, doctor…and thank you," Joe said. Andie ran over and gave the doctor a quick hug. Dr. Weinstein laughed and said, "Well, that's not necessary. You go and rest now, okay?"

As Andie and Joe stepped out of the vet's office, they heard the door locking behind them. They wearily walked the few steps to the restaurant, each thinking their own private thoughts of the day behind them, and the day to come.

Having said their good-nights to June and watched as she turned off the lights and locked the front door, Andie and Joe climbed the creaky wood stairs to the upstairs apartment. Streetlights shining through the front windows shed just enough brightness to light their way. They reached a wooden door, which Joe opened, and they entered the unfamiliar room. A small kitchen light shone into three small rooms, the living area, the bedroom and the aforementioned kitchen.

Andie walked into the kitchen and opened the refrigerator. "Huh. I guess June made sure we had something to eat," she said. "It looks like we have a few wrapped sandwiches and a couple of sodas."

Andie closed the fridge door then sat down at a small table with two chairs. "That was nice of her."

Joe wiped a hand across his tired face. "Sure, but I think I need to get some shut-eye. It's been a long day, you know?"

Andie gave him a small sympathetic smile. "Yes, I do. Let's check out the accommodations."

They walked towards the bedroom and stopped at the door.

"A double bed," Andie commented. "And no couch in the living room."

Joe nodded.

"Let's just sleep in the bed. I don't mind sharing, if you don't," Andie offered.

Joe merely nodded again. He sat on the edge of the bed and removed his shoes.

Andie walked to the bathroom in the hallway and splashed cold water on her face. She didn't bother turning on the light. It didn't matter what she looked like. It didn't matter that her clothes were rumpled and stained in places with Satchmo's blood. Nothing really mattered right then, except sleep. She walked back to the bedroom, where she saw Joe partially under the covers, fully dressed, and snoring. She slipped onto the bed and soon joined Joe in oblivious sleep.

Several hours later, Andie startled awake with a gasp. She turned her head to find Joe wide awake, staring at the ceiling. "Are you okay?" he asked.

Andie swallowed, and took a deep breath. "It must have been a bad dream. I don't know…" She shook her head.

"This has all been a bad dream," Joe said. "A bad freaking dream that just looks like its never going to end."

Andie arranged herself under the blanket. "I agree. It's like an episode of the Twilight Zone."

"Only it's real. And if we're not careful, we could die," Joe said.

"At least the aliens haven't come to this town yet."

"They will. It's only a matter of time," Joe warned.

"But I think for now we have to take advantage of the fact that they're not here. We need to figure out where we're going to stay, and how we're going to live," Andie said.

"Well, for now, we're staying put. I'm not leaving until Satchmo heals. If he survives, that is," Joe's voice caught in this throat.

"He will," Andie said. "I just feel that in my bones. Dr. Weinstein seemed like someone we could trust."

"Depends on how bad Satch was hurt," Joe continued.

Andie reached over and placed her hand on Joe's forearm. "Don't torture yourself. We won't know anything until morning." She thought for a moment, then asked, "How long have you had Satch?"

"I got him when he was a pup, about eight years ago. He's an old man, now, but he was quite a terror in his early days," Joe said.

Andie laughed, "Oh, I can imagine. He certainly has a strong personality."

"Yeah," Joe chuckled. "One minute he's sleeping on my shoes, the next he's chewing off someone's leg."

"He is loyal to you."

"Oh, yeah, friends to the end."

"So, you got him when you were in high school?"

"College. He was my best buddy. Helped me pick up the girls," Joe said with a wry twist of his lips. "I was living in an off-campus apartment, and I wanted someone to protect my things when I was at classes. I didn't trust my roommates not to help themselves to my stuff."

"And was he a good guard dog?"

"Ha!" Joe's laughter exploded, and he turned on his side to face Andie. "He wanted to play with the guys all day. I'd come home and he'd be pulling off someone's sock or begging for a treat. The guys really liked him."

"And because they were so occupied with Satchmo's antics, they didn't mess with your stuff," Andie noted.

Joe smiled, "Well, hey, I guess you're right. I never thought of it that way."

"Why didn't you live in the dorms? When I went to the University of Connecticut, I loved living in the coed dorms."

"I can tell you're more social than I am. I prefer a few people at a time. The dorms just seemed a bit too wild and wooly for me."

Now it was Andie's turn to laugh, "Wooly? What does that even mean?"

"It means crazy, I guess," Joe said.

"That's true. The dorms could get a bit nuts at times when the students needed to blow off steam, like after exams."

"College seems like a lifetime ago," Joe said. "Hell, last week seems like a lifetime ago." He stared off into the dark. "Remember when we could just walk outside and not have to worry about aliens or psychos or death or the end of the world?"

"I do," Andie said. "It was just a few days ago. And it's going to be okay again, someday."

Joe stared into the light reflecting from Andie's eyes. "You make it seem as if things will be alright. You always put a positive spin on things."

"I'm trying, Joe," Andie whispered. There were several long moments of silence, then Joe leaned towards her. "I want to kiss you," he said.

"Okay," she barely spoke. The tension between them was palpable. It would only be relieved by the touch of Joe's soft lips on hers. Within seconds, their arms encircled each other. Their kisses deepened until there was the urge to go further. Joe reached slightly down under the covers to caress Andie's breast. She shivered, but then gasped and pulled away.

"Joe!" she cried out. "Stop." She sat up straight, holding the sheets against her body. "I don't even know you. You don't know me. I don't do this kind of thing."

Joe pulled away from Andie to the edge of the bed. He ran a hand through his rumpled hair. "Come on, Andie. What's the problem? We felt an attraction. We're two consenting adults."

Andie shook her head. "No. This isn't good. We need to keep our heads in the right place. We need to survive. Not fool around as if we didn't have a care in the world."

Joe closed his eyes and responded. "Andie, in the history of the world, people have turned to each other for comfort during times of trouble. It's human nature."

Andie's face contorted and then a tear escaped one corner of her eyes. "I know. I get that." She pulled in a deep breath, and continued. "But I don't want to do something against my nature. I don't sleep with someone unless I care for them, unless I have a relationship. And we don't have that. We are two people who've been thrown together in the midst of an alien invasion."

Joe groaned then ruefully smiled at Andie. "All right. But let it be said that you agreed to my kiss."

"I did," Andie said. "And I will admit I got carried away. I'm not blaming anyone for my own behavior."

"That's good. And now we know that we have to be more careful in the future." Joe looked Andie in the eyes. "But you don't know what you're missing."

Andie laughed and felt that perhaps their relationship could return to solid footing. She extended a hand to Joe, "Friends?"

"Friends," he replied.

# CHAPTER 15

As the darkness of the night turned to dawn, Andie and Joe woke refreshed. Joe ran down to the car to retrieve some clothing for each of them while Andie jumped into the shower. After dressing, and placing her dirty clothing from the day before into a plastic bag she found in the small upstairs kitchen, Andie ventured downstairs to the restaurant. She found June humming to herself in the large industrial kitchen.

"Hey," Andie called.

"Oh!" June cried. "You scared me, girl." June had whipped around with a spatula held high in the air in attack mode. She brought the spatula down and into a mixture on the stove. "I'm always thinking anything that moves is going to be one of those blasted monsters."

"I'm sorry about that, June," Andie said. "Can I help you in here? What's cooking?"

"I'm making a big batch of scrambled eggs, and I thought I'd throw on some bacon. How's that sound?"

"Excellent!" Andie responded. "I feel like I'm starving, even though I ate that burger and fries last night."

"It's okay. The body knows when it needs nourishment. Why don't you slap some bacon on the griddle, and I'll make some toast to go with the eggs."

"You got it," Andie pulled the raw bacon from the fridge and then placed six pieces on the already-warmed griddle. "Oh, heck," she muttered, and then added six more slices. As the bacon sizzled, and the eggs thickened, the wholesome, homey smells wafted through the kitchen and lifted Andie's spirits. When Joe entered the kitchen whistling and tucking his shirt into his jeans, he commented, "This place smells like heaven."

June called out, "Joe, can you get some juice from the fridge and pour everyone a glass?"

"Sure," Joe said, and set upon his task.

Within minutes, with everything ready to be served and eaten, June shooed Joe and Andie into the dining room where they all sat at a big table with chairs in the center of the room. "This is usually our party table," June announced. "Let's live it up."

June surprised the others with homemade biscuits that she had made earlier, and that had been warming in the oven. Altogether, it was a breakfast feast that gave them comfort and allowed them a few minutes of joy. Andie considered that happiness could be found in the most unusual times and places, even a diner in an unfamiliar town.

June and Andie cleaned up the dining room and kitchen while Joe went out to take a short walk around the town. It was still too early for the vet to be open. Andie settled into reading more of her Ray Bradbury novel, finding some escape in the tale of the young boy who lived among fascinating people in ordinary times. She sat in a booth near the back of the restaurant, sipping coffee, and greeting the customer or two who wandered in for breakfast.

As Andie was reading, she overheard two older men conversing in a booth behind hers. She tried to block out the voices, but it grew impossible as the men began to argue.

"I'm telling you, Clifford. We need to take our wives and get the heck out of here. It's not going to be long before the spacemen come. And then what are we going to do? Nobody is here to protect us! We're in the middle of nowhere!"

"But that's what I'm saying, Lewis. If we stay here, we're going to be safer because nobody, including the spacemen, knows we're here. They have bigger fish to fry in places like New York City and Washington, D.C." The man slapped his hands on the tabletop. "If we go somewhere with lots of people, we'll be goners for sure!"

"I get what you're saying, Clifford, but the wife wants to be with her grandkids. How am I supposed to fight that?" Lewis exhaled in exasperation.

Clifford sighed. "Lewis, you've got to put your foot down and tell the missus that you're staying right here."

"Easy for you to say," Lewis muttered. "You're not married to Susie."

Andie put her book on the table, face down to the open page. She cleared her throat loudly several times until she got the attention of the two older men.

"Listen, guys? Can I say something?" Andie said.

"Sure, missy," said Clifford, the more friendly-seeming of the two.

"I think you should stay here," Andie said. "I mean here or somewhere in the park. I just came from D.C. yesterday, and it's a mess. The alien discs are killing people left and right, anyone that moves. It's almost impossible to drive the highways because of all the crashes. At least here, you're safe for the time being, and you can come up with a plan in case the aliens do make it here."

Clifford nodded. "That's what I've been saying to my friend here. We should get our gear and head into the woods. We can hide out there."

Lewis groaned. "We're senior citizens, not boy scouts! I can't make Susie live in a tent!"

"Of course, you can! We can go get some of those fancy tents with all the bells and whistles. Susie will think she's at a four-star hotel." Clifford started to stand up from the table.

"Thanks, young lady. You've given me the motivation I needed to get myself organized. First, I'm going to the grocery store and buying all the canned goods we'll need for a few months. Then I'm going to the camping store and get the best tent money will buy." He turned to his friend who was still seated with his head in his hands. "Are you with me, Lewis?"

Lewis looked up at his friend, and wincing, said, "I guess so. I'm not going to be the one to bust this 40-year- old friendship. But you're the one who's going to have to carry Susie with us, screaming and kicking all the way."

"I'm sure glad I married Donna. She's not going to give me any trouble. In fact, she'll think it's a hoot." The two men turned to Andie and said their good-byes. Andie hoped that she had done the right thing in encouraging the men not to travel elsewhere. She idly hoped that she and Joe might run into the couples when they themselves had settled into the parklands. As she reached to pick up her book and continue reading, Joe entered the restaurant, setting off the chimes and making his presence known to all within.

# *CHAPTER 16*

Andie stood and met Joe halfway from the door. "Is Satchmo okay? Have you talked to the vet?" she asked.

Joe nodded, "Dr. Weinstein says Satch is doing well. He's still being medicated so that he'll lie still while he recuperates. It might be a day or two before we can have him back."

Andie nodded. "That's good. Thank God." Andie looked upwards as if thanking the heavens for this news.

Joe smiled. "And here I thought you believed everything was going to be okay. What's with the God stuff?"

"It never hurts to have a back-up," Andie sniffed with her reply.

"Let's go sit down," Joe said. "I have something to tell you."

"Oh?" Andie felt a frisson of fear at his words, but took a seat in the nearest booth. "Shoot," she said.

"Funny you should say that because shooting is exactly what this is about." Joe took a deep breath and then met Andie's eyes. "When I was walking around town, I went to the mayor's office. They're still staffed with a few people. Anyway, Mayor Wilson was there, and I was able to tell him about what happened on Skyline Drive."

"Uh-huh," Andie commented, watching the stern expression on Joe's face.

"The mayor and some of the other folks in town want to go and clean out that hornet's nest up at Skyland. They've heard rumors before, but my story was the first one they heard in-person. So now they're rounding up any able-bodied man or woman who can shoot a gun, and we're heading up there this afternoon."

"We, huh? So, you're going to join this posse to relive the shootout at the OK Corral. I don't like it. We both know those guys at Skyland are armed and dangerous. I need you. Satchmo needs you."

"So, you're playing the Satchmo card, are you? Okay, maybe I downplayed the situation. But these people are determined to keep the peace in these parts, and I feel a duty to join them. Because of Satchmo. I can play that card, too."

Andie ran her hands through her hair. "Fine. But be careful, Joe. Come back so that we can fight the other bad guys."

Joe's brow crumpled in confusion. "The other bad guys?"

"The aliens, Joe, the friggin' aliens." Andie sighed. She shook her head and then smiled.

They filled the next few hours with checking on Satchmo, who was unconscious but doing well, collecting additional camping materials from the local outfitters and discussing future plans, with June's knowledgeable input of the area. Midafternoon, Joe set off with his gun to join the mayor and his group of vigilantes. Andie took a walk through the quiet town streets, staying on alert for any stray moving black discs. She thought she might like to live in such a gentle, homey place someday. Maybe when she retired, she thought. But then she shook her head and laughed at herself. That's if she survived the coming alien onslaught. The alien discs were probably going to be easy compared to what the distant threat that was headed to Earth could offer.

After she returned to Ed's Diner, Joe entered a few minutes later, dirty and with ripped pants legs, but apparently unharmed.

"Joe!" yelled Andie across the empty restaurant, save for June, who was seated at a table with her in the back. Andie got up and ran through the tables and chairs and grabbed Joe in a hard hug. "Are you okay?" She stepped back to make a full assessment.

"Fit as a fiddle," Joe said while slapping his hands on his arms and legs to prove his wholeness. "Though I can't say the same for that Skyland gang. We got them all, Andie. Buck and his buddies are locked up and will be sent to the closest prison when they've been arraigned."

Andie grinned. "Vengeance for Satchmo has been served!"

June proclaimed, "That calls for a round of iced teas!" She added, "We don't serve liquor here."

Andie and Joe laughed and settled into the wood chairs at the table as June headed to the kitchen.

"Satchmo's good," Andie commented. "I checked on him just before you got back. The doc has him awake now."

"That's great news!" Joe said.

"It gets better," Andie said. "The doc said we can have Satch back tomorrow. He'll give us the meds and bandages that we'll need for the next few weeks."

Joe breathed in quickly. "That's so fast. Is the doc sure Satch doesn't need a few more days in the clinic?"

"Well, the doc feels certain we can handle the leg. We just need to be observant and careful." Andie tilted her head. "And…the doc is leaving town tomorrow, so that option no longer exists."

Joe nodded. "I see. Well, I don't blame Doc Weinstein, what with the violence up on the Drive and the impending aliens. He's just doing what we all are-trying to stay safe in the best way he knows how."

Andie reached over and grasped Joe's hand. "I get it. I really do."

"So tomorrow we'll get back up on Skyline Drive. The guys at the camping store mentioned a hunting shack down one of the overgrown side roads. If we can't find that, maybe we can look for some stone structures, some logs, somewhere. One of those abandoned houses that the mountain people left behind.  I really don't know. It's a shot in the dark."

Andie nodded again. "Yes, but we'll do it together, you, me and Satch. Like the Three Musketeers."

"All for one, and one for all."

# *CHAPTER 17*

With the car packed so tightly that no sunlight came through the back windows, they took off at first light. Andie left a note for June, thanking her for the friendship and food. It felt as if they were sneaking away, but neither Joe or Andie had been able to rest well the night before, each consumed with thoughts of an undetermined and unpredictable future. They wanted and needed to get to their destination, wherever that might be.

Joe took the wheel while Andie sat beside him, Satchmo resting in her lap. The sun, already bright in the clear skies, seemed a token of good fortune. But then Andie laughed to herself as she considered that she was being foolish thinking that luck could exist in such an upside-down world filled with killer aliens and spaceships.

"The guy at the store said we need to look for a sort-of clearing, with an orange ribbon tied to a sapling on each side of the road opening," Joe said. "Apparently there is a lot of overgrowth on the road, so it barely can be seen, but the ribbons may help us."

The car had left the small town and traveled on to Skyline Drive. Joe drove slowly, only occasionally passing another car going in the opposite direction.

"More people today," Andie observed.

"I would think that it has to be getting rougher in the suburbs. People are trying to escape," Joe said.

"Like us," Andie murmured. "At least we got in some lead time. That helped us with knowing where to look for shelters."

"The difference is we are going to escape, not just try," Joe stated.

Andie nodded, and offered a silent prayer for their little ragtag group.

"Were you just praying?" Joe asked. He turned for a quick glimpse of her face.

Andie rolled her eyes with an exaggerated sigh. "Yes. Even though I don't consider myself religious by any means, I sometimes feel prayer helps. You can pray to God, nature, the winds, whatever, but it comforts me and maybe some deity or being will listen and answer."

Joe laughed. "Where was your deity when Satchmo was attacked?"

Andie stiffened. "I didn't say it was a given. Geez, that was kind of cruel, Joe." She tried to relax her body as Satchmo made a sound while he reclined in her lap.

Joe checked his rearview mirror then scanned the terrain ahead. After a few minutes, he said, "I'm sorry, Andie. I just feel like we're living on the edge, and the thought of a benevolent God or gods is far from reality right now."

"That's funny," Andie said as she gritted her teeth. "I feel that we need a caring god more than ever. Who else is going to save us from this horror show?"

"We are. We are going to save ourselves," Joe gripped the wheel tighter.

"Orange ribbons!" Andie shouted. "I saw orange ribbons back there. Turn around."

Joe screeched to a halt in the road, and turned to look backwards.

"I saw them, Joe," Andie said, "Don't you believe me?" She stared at him in disbelief.

"Just a gut reaction. I believe you," Joe said. He began to turn the car around, checking for any oncoming traffic in either direction. He edged towards the spot where Andie had noted the orange ribbons.

"There!" she shouted and pointed to the trees on their left side. Sure enough, a faded orange ribbon waved in the slight breeze.

"Good call, but I see only one ribbon," Joe noted.

"Maybe one got untied and fell into the brush. I'll go look." Joe pulled over to the side of the road while Andie unbuckled her seatbelt. She transferred Satchmo to her seat as she eased out of the car. Looking in both directions, she ran across the road and searched in the tangled grass. After a few moments, Andie held up a muddied orange ribbon and waved it towards Joe.

He rolled down his window, and called, "Stay there. I'll pull down the road." From Andie's viewpoint, it was more a path than a road. It definitely wasn't paved, and tall weeds and brambles twisted in every direction. Joe inched his way onto the forgotten road and drove down a few feet until the car was safely off the main drive. He shut down the car and got out.

"This is wild," he said shaking his head. "Where's the cabin?"

Andie pointed down a slight slope. "I bet it's around the corner down there. Want me to go and check?"

"No. Stay with Satch. I'll be right back." Joe began hiking down the pathway, pushing aside fallen tree limbs and stepping around rocks in case of snakes. As he turned the corner in the path, he spotted the cabin a few yards away. It was made of rough timber, and the roof needed some reinforcement, but it seemed sturdy enough for their purposes. About twenty yards away from the cabin, he saw a creek rushing among jagged rocks. "Okay, so there is a god," he said to himself.

Joe climbed back uphill and caught Andie sitting in her passenger seat, stroking Satchmo's head. "It's all good," he said to her. "Let's go for it." He got into the car and drove the bumpy and treacherous road until he came to a stop in front of the small cabin.

"There's no place like home," Andie recited as she turned to smile at Joe.

"Be it ever so humble…" Joe joined in. Andie laughed and once again slid out of the car. Joe joined her at the cabin's door. She pushed the heavy wood door open, and they stepped into the shelter. A small window in the side wall gave them enough light to see the roughhewn chairs and table. A bed with a questionable mattress sat against the opposite wall. There were cupboards filled with a few plates, utensils and even several mugs. A small stone fireplace was built into the back wall with a cooking pot suspended from rods in the stonework.

Andie turned around in a circle several times, assessing the situation and noting its good features as well as imperfections. "We'll have to cover the window most of the time for safety. Those discs are going to make their way here. And, of course, everything will have to be dusted and cleaned before we empty the car."

Joe nodded, and said, "Let me get some cloths and sponges from the car. Satch can rest on the bed for now."

"We'll have to make him a dog bed," Andie noted.

"Sure," Joe said. "But first things first." He left and then quickly returned with Satchmo in his strong arms. Satch opened one eye, grunted, then fell back to sleep as soon as Joe settled him on the bed.

"He approves," said Andie.

"He's drunk on the pain meds," Joe said.

"You can be a pain," Andie said.

"So you've told me before." Joe sighed. He brought the cleaning items into the cabin. "Where do I start?"

"How about the fireplace? You can clean out any old ashes and check the flue."

"I'll do my best. I've never messed around with a fireplace before. I'm just an IT guy from Columbia."

"And I'm a teacher from Columbia, but that and a dollar with get you a cup of coffee." Andie began to wipe and dust the surfaces, but soon realized that she needed water to clean more thoroughly. She quizzically looked around the room. "Hey, there's no faucet or sink. How do we get water?"

Joe laughed, "Did you notice that creek as we came in? That's our water source. I'll go get the bucket I picked up at the store and bring some back."

As he left, Andie had another thought. Where would they go to the bathroom? In the woods behind the cabin? They were going to have to build an outhouse. She slowly sat down on the mattress with Satchmo, feeling defeated and tired, even though it was only mid-morning. "I don't know if I can do this, Satch." She frowned, and then added, "No, I *can* do this, but I don't want to. See the difference?" Satchmo didn't open an eye.

Andie returned to cleaning and organizing, her efforts much improved by the fresh cold water from the creek. Joe poked into the chimney, turned a knob he found on the stone surrounding and claimed he saw some daylight as he peered upwards.

"You're my hero," Andie teased. Joe bowed to her praise. She just rolled her eyes.

"Hey, I'm hungry. Let's break for lunch before we unload the car," Andie said.

"Sounds great. I'll get the sandwiches June packed for us last night." Andie gratefully sank into one of the large chairs at the table while she waited for Joe. Now that the cabin was clean, she felt a little better about their situation. She knew how close she had been to having to survive in a pile of stones left over from decades ago.

They ate their roast beef sandwiches and chips like two starving wolves.

"Listen, Andie?" Joe asked. "I want to do something that is going to leave you to empty the car on your own."

Andie raised her gaze to stare at Joe. "Oh?"

"Um, yes. I think I need to go back up the hill and cover our tracks. Make it look like no one drove in. And take down the one orange ribbon."

Andie nodded in agreement. "That's an excellent idea. We don't need any uninvited visitors."

"That's what I thought. I'll use a big branch to whack at the underbrush to make it seem all wild and wooly, like it was before."

"There's that wild and wooly again. Okay, then! Let's get to work." Andie swept up the paper wrappers from the sandwiches, and then realizing there was no garbage can, left them in the middle of the table.

Joe pointed to the trash on the table. "About that, we can use a plastic bag for trash in the cabin for now. But we'll have to dig holes and bury trash now and then. We need to keep the bears away, too."

"Oh my god-bears," Andie moaned. She was extra cautious as she walked to the car and pulled out some packed boxes of dry food. It was hard to believe that just a few days ago she was living in Columbia, Maryland, unaware of what a nightmare life would become. So much death, and poor sweet

Miss Bey as probably one of the countless millions to be destroyed by a fierce death ray.

The hard work took Andie's mind off all the suffering as she filled the cabin with the food and gear they needed to survive. She was glad she had packed some books, as had Joe, and looked forward to escaping into more Ray Bradbury novels.

A few hours later, Joe returned, exhausted and covered in dried leaves and prickles. He scooped some water from the bucket with a mug and gulped it down.

"That should do it," he remarked, looking around the room, appraising the ways Andie had furnished and stored items in all available spaces and crannies. "Hey, you did a nice job."

"High praise from you, Joe," Andie smiled. "And thanks for hiding our tracks."

"I think I did an okay job. I'll go back tomorrow to check."

"Yes, and could we, um, start building an outhouse?" Andie asked meekly.

"Does a bear sh--. Never mind. We also need to camouflage this cabin. It looks like a place where people live. We need to turn it into something organic-looking."

Andie stood, looking puzzled. "Hmm. I need to think about this. Maybe I could braid vines and stems that we could hang from the roof. And the roof could be covered with branches and stuff."

"That's tomorrow's problem. Let's have a toast with some warm soda I managed to stow away. "

"Coke?" Andie asked hopefully.

"Of course."

"Let me at it!"

"Coming right up!" Joe pretended to scurry from the cabin as Andie lay down on the bed with Satchmo.

"Yes, tomorrow is another day." Andie was too tired even to smile as she recalled the words of Scarlett O'Hara. "We're not in Kansas anymore. And I might be going crazy," she said.

# *CHAPTER 18*

Andie awoke the next morning with a start. It took a moment to realize where she was. Then it took another second to understand what woke her. It was a sound, coming from outside the window. The window they hadn't covered yet. Andie tried to breathe, but her heart was beating so fast she could scarcely pull air into her lungs. The sound was unusual, like something was bumping up against the cabin. It moved along the side of the cabin, and then slowly began to edge toward the front.

Andie nudged Joe. "Joe, Joe!" she whispered.

Joe, lying beside her in the bed under his own sleeping bag, opened one eye and answered, "I hear it. Don't move."

"Could it be the aliens? Are they here?"

"I don't know, and I don't want to find out. Just lay there and be quiet."

Andie sucked in a breath and listened as the noise came closer to their door, just feet away from the foot of their bed. Suddenly, there was a huge bang and the door popped open. Andie jumped from the bed and ran to push the door closed. She stayed pressed against it, with her feet planted wide on the floor for balance. "Oh my god, help me," she pleaded.

Joe had already tossed aside his covers and made a leap across the room to join Andie at the door. Whatever was behind the door pushed against it again. Andie looked at Joe, her eyes wide with fear.

"Just stay here. Don't move. It will be fine," Joe softly spoke to calm her down. They remained side by side, pushing against the door with all their strength, for what seemed like a lifetime, but was probably only a few minutes. Then they heard a scuffling sound as the noise moved again to the side of the cabin. They raised their eyes to the window, as a tall buck with pointed antlers sauntered by.

"It was a deer. A damn deer." Andie slid down to the floor with her back against the door. "I can't believe it. We almost had a deer in the cabin."

She started to giggle, and then began to laugh helplessly as the relief overcame her.

Joe slid down next to her and joined in the laughter. "If it isn't the aliens, then it's the wildlife that's going to get you."

"I thought we were going to die," Andie said after the wave of laughter settled into rolling giggles.

"You were stinking amazing. You jumped from the bed and over to the door like the Flash. I couldn't believe it." Joe looked at her in admiration.

"Yeah, I was kinda going on adrenaline power. All motion and no thoughts." She was just glad it had been a deer and not a bear.

"Well, let me tell you. If I have to be stuck in the woods, with my medicated bulldog and all kinds of shit coming after us, I'm glad it's you by my side," Joe declared.

Andie nodded. "Same here. And that was a really sweet thing to say."

Joe stared at her face, her full lips, her wild bedhead hair, and gave an embarrassed smile. He was experiencing feelings that were better left hidden. "Yeah, well, don't get used to it, girl. Now let's get up and at 'em! There's a window to be covered and a door needing a few latches to keep out rude animals."

After a breakfast of oranges and dry Fruit Loops, they got back into the rhythm of working. Joe had finally woken Satchmo who was still functioning in a dazed state on his own soft sleeping bag. Satch slurped fresh water from his bowl and even tried some soft dog food before collapsing back down into his cozy nest.

"I'm going to cut down the pain med dosage. He seems to be feeling much better." Joe said. "He needs to start moving a bit or he's going to be awfully stiff."

"Not to mention, he's going to have to go to the bathroom outside soon. No more doggie diapers for him," Andie noted.

"We'll have to stay with him whenever he's outside. He might make a nice meal for some predator, and I'm not going to let that happen."

"Ditto," said Andie, as she taped a white cloth to the window. Some light still came through, but it dimmed the room considerably.

After Joe hammered some crude wood pieces to the door that would adequately serve as door locks for protection, he went out to the car where some of the equipment was still stacked in the trunk. He pulled out the solar- powered radio and weather station and opened the solar panels. It was a bright sunny early spring day, so the device would be ready for use in a few hours. Joe needed to hear what was happening in the world. He needed to learn how far the aliens had infiltrated the cities and towns. Was anyone leading the fight against the aliens, and had they found a way to destroy them?

Joe began to gather loose branches and twigs from the edge of the woods and threw them into a pile beside the cabin. Andie heard some strange noises overhead while she organized the cabin. She walked outdoors to find Joe tossing up the tree branches to cover the cabin's roof. She joined in, and together they made slow but steady progress in turning the cabin into an arbor. It didn't take long before they became tired and drenched in sweat.

"Let's go to the stream," Joe said. "We can cool down with a refreshing dip."

"Ha!" Andie responded. "A dip into the freezing cold mountain water? I'll maybe poke my feet into the water, but that's it." She picked her way among the tall grass to stand at the edge of the creek. "This is truly beautiful."

"And its all ours, fish included, for the duration of our visit." Joe sat down and pulled off his sneakers. "All we have to do is catch them. How are you at filleting fish?"

"I've done it. I'll make us some fried fish over the fire. How about fish stew? Would you eat that?" Andie asked.

"Sure. The way we're working these days, a nice hearty fish stew would go down nicely."

Andie sat down on the hard packed earth of the creek's bank. She watched as Joe took off his shoes, and then started to pull down his jeans.

"Hey, mister!" Andie called. "No funny stuff allowed on this beach." She turned her head away.

"I'm wading in whether you like it or not. I wear boxers so there's nothing naked going on. And, by the way, my boxers have the Batman symbol on them, which I happen to know you like."

Andie tentatively turned her head back to observe Joe in his colorful boxer shorts. She shook her head in chagrin. "That is so nerdy."

Joe laughed, then waded into the creek until he was covered to his waist. "Now this feels like heaven. You should try it, Andie."

"Nope. Not until the temperature gets over 75 or 80. I have my standards to uphold," Andie said.

"Well, I'll be able to let you know when that happens. I have the solar radio and temp gauge powering up even as we speak."

They remained quiet for a few minutes, each lost in their various thoughts. The gentle warmth of the sun beat down, making them feel safe and alive. Joe soon felt the chill of the icy water, and waded out of the stream.

"Look away, Andie. I'm going to take off these wet shorts and put on my jeans."

Andie caught an eyeful of the water streaming down Joe's well-proportioned body, then quickly darted her eyes to the side.

"Thanks for the warning. I wouldn't want to be subjected to your naked bod." But to herself she added, 'Even though it's quite all that.'

Joe dressed and then sprawled out beside Andie on the sandy bank of the creek. "This feels like a little bit of heaven," he murmured as he shut his eyes and felt the rays caressing his face.

"We are so lucky to have found this place. I mean, it's not a five-star hotel, but for our purposes, it is kinda perfect." Andie enjoyed the breeze that lifted her hair and danced across her face.

"I can't believe the guys at the sports store told me about it. That just doesn't happen in the real world."

"Well, they weren't going to be using it, right? So, they figured why not share it with the nice guy from Columbia? Small town folks sometimes have more solid values," Andie decided.

"I guess. It didn't hurt that I paid them a fortune for all the camping stuff I got there. They weren't going to be having many more customers since the town had pretty much emptied out."

"Still. It was good of them," Andie persisted.

"Well, sure," Joe said.

The sound of the rushing water relaxed them, along with the chirps of frogs in the nearby grasses and birds high in the birch trees.

"All that nightmare stuff with the aliens feels far away from here," Andie stated. "Don't you think?"

"For now, it does," Joe said.

"And what happened to Satch seems like weeks ago, instead of days." She stared at the streams of sunlight shining through ripples of water. "Do you think we did the right thing by coming here to these mountains? Maybe the northern mountains would have been better, less risky?" Andie was again feeling the guilt of her choice to travel south.

"Oh, Andie. That's a question that has no answers. We made the decision based on some quick research and following our gut feelings. There's nothing that says we were right or wrong. What happened was beyond our knowing."

"Yeah. I get that. But I still feel responsible for Miss Bey and Satchmo." Andie sighed deeply. "I've never had such fallout from a decision I made."

"I feel responsible, too. But we weren't the ones who hurt them, Andie. We have to remember that."

"When this is all over, there might be a church and some confessions in my future," Andie said.

"Whatever gets you through the day," said Joe. He turned over to let the sun warm his back.

"I guess I'm wondering how long we'll be here. Through the spring, maybe the summer? But what if the aliens stay and we have to hide out through the cold weather? All we have is the cooking fireplace for heat. And we will definitely be out of food by then." Andie picked a blade of grass and began to fashion it into a whistle.

"The way I see it," said Joe, "we'll do just fine. We'll fish for food, maybe even hunt if we get hungry enough. We will find nuts and berries. My old boy scouting days will come in handy."

Andie smiled at him as he turned his head to make eye contact. "We'll be like Ma and Pa in Little House on the Prairie. Except with no kids."

Joe laughed, "All in due time."

"What!" Andie's eyes popped with surprise. "There will be no kids coming into this scenario. You can count on that," she huffed.

"I was just taking your Ma and Pa comments a little further," he said. "If we have to stay through a winter, I predict that we're going to have to cuddle up to keep warm. And…one thing could lead to another."

"I can't even begin to answer that comment," Andie said. "We made it through last night without any of your so-called cuddling."

"It wasn't freezing last night," Joe said.

"Maybe the cold will make the aliens incapable of functioning," Andie wondered. She spotted a trout jumping from the water upstream.

Joe shook his head in chagrin. "I hope something does before the winter. There has to be something that they can't withstand. Like in the movies, maybe there's some dust or allergen that makes them break down."

"I sure hope the world's governments are working together to figure this out," Andie stated.

"If the world leaders survive. But I imagine most are in airtight bunkers at this point."

Andie threw down her piece of grass. "But why are they after us humans? Why not the animals and all the other living things?"

"It's not like Earth is a prize in the popcorn box. We've allowed the Earth to become polluted. The oceans are filled with plastics. Global warming is destroying the icecaps. There are a million small repercussions for our negligent behavior that are leading this planet into a wasteland. So why would they want it? Or do they just hate humans in general? Maybe they have a prime directive to kill all intelligent lifeforms."

"I always wanted to see aliens in my lifetime. Now that they're here, I wish they were gone," Andie said.

"Well, first we have yet to meet any aliens. You've seen some eyes, and we've only seen their weapons and saucers. And second, you had to know that the chances were slim that another species would be kind and welcoming," Joe said.

"A lot of the science fiction novels I've read were based on first contact and then developing a relationship with the other beings," Andie said.

Joe laughed. "And a lot of the other science fiction novels had creepy green men that wanted to abduct us or kill us."

"I know. I just want us to survive so that we can see the end of this. I want to know the reasons. I want to be able to see a future where we can begin again. Maybe join up with others who somehow survive."

"Sort of starting a brave new world? Maybe." Joe rubbed his feet in the soft soil on the edge of the stream.

"I sure hope the aliens aren't going to stay here. Then our chances are pretty slim, no matter what we do. It's going to take a while for the discs to find everyone, so I think we have some time. But ultimately, it's not looking good." Andie didn't want to face this truth, but she felt it was necessary.

Joe sat up. "Wow, Andie. This conversation took a wide turn. We started off feeling happy with our little cabin by the stream and ended up admitting to our ultimate destruction. It's a lot to take in, and I'm starving. Let's rustle up a meal and see how Satchmo is doing. I bet he's awake and wondering where the heck he is."

Andie stood up and almost lost her balance on an uneven rock surface, but Joe grabbed her arm and steadied her.

"Whoa, partner! Let's keep both feet on the ground at all times."

Andie giggled. "My ex-boyfriend's mother used to say that when I visited him in his bedroom."

"Living with his mother? How charming," Joe remarked.

"Yes, but at least she was a fantastic cook. As you'll find out, I am not."

# *CHAPTER 19*

Andie was sitting on the cabin floor, petting Satchmo, who was preening with the attention. He was getting back to his normal adorable self, but he was still unable to stand on his hind legs for more than a few seconds. Dr. Weinstein had told them that the process of healing would take a few weeks at best so he was catered to for his every need and desire. Joe had squirreled away a large bag of doggie treats, and Andie made sure that Satchmo was given his fill. She couldn't believe how much she loved this dog. He was an older sort of canine but it made Andie love him all the more. His bravery at the lodge had shown Andie that courage comes in all forms, human and animal, and she would respect Satchmo and all other living creatures more than she ever had before.

Andie bent down and kissed one of Satchmo's silky ears. "You are a good dog, Satch. Maybe even the best dog."

Satchmo thumped his tail. Andie could see the effort that caused him and stroked his back to soothe him. "It's okay. You just take it easy, boy."

Suddenly, she heard Joe calling from outside the cabin. "Andie, come here!"

"What?" she called as she stood up.

"Just get out here, please," Joe asked in a strident tone.

"Your master calls," Andie said to Satch as she opened the cabin door and peered out. Joe was several feet away in the late afternoon sunlight, crouched next to the solar radio.

"I think I got something on the radio," he said. "I've been trying for hours, and there's been nothing but static. Did the aliens attack the power grids?"

Andie kneeled in the grass next to him. "But you heard something?"

"Yeah. Hang on." Joe fiddled with the knobs. turning the volume louder and sliding a few millimeters down the dial past several stations. Then, there it was. Unmistakable human speech, sometimes broken by static, but definitely broadcasting.

"The scientists at NASA Space Center have confirmed that the lights we've seen at night are indeed a type of space flotilla, and they are headed towards our planet. It appears that there are approximately 50 space vessels, each the size of Manhattan. The best estimate for arrival in Earth's orbit, based on their current rate of travel, is five days from today. It can be understood how the smaller invader spacecraft were enabled to arrive here, now that we have seen the motherships. Various government officials around the world have indicated that this is a serious threat to our survival. They have advised that citizens based in the cities find shelter elsewhere where chances of escaping this enemy may be more successful. It is predicted that the larger alien vessels will either remain in space above major cities where human population is dense or land in or next to cities. This is based on the current behavior of the small alien craft and the alien discs which are terrorizing humans. It is felt that the intruders will stop at nothing to eradicate humans from the surface of the planet. For those of you in remote areas, you may find it hard to believe the death toll that is occurring in most cities and suburbs in America. With the demise of so many people and the fear of those who have managed to survive this apocalypse, all private and public businesses and services have been affected. There are few television, cable or radio stations still broadcasting. This station will continue for as long as we are safe, but we are only a handful who wish to help when and where we can. God bless, and let's keep fighting the good fight."

Static overtook the radio station, and Joe quickly turned down the volume. "Let's keep the radio set on this station. Maybe we can check it again tomorrow to see if there are any updates.

"They certainly didn't mince words about the aliens," Andie said.

"Nope. They gave us the facts, and it's up to us to figure out what we want to do with it."

"Alien bastards."

Andie sat back and stared into the woods. She wondered if her family, her friends, even policeman Frank, were still alive. She felt so far away from everyone she had known, as they hid in the Allegheny Mountains. She also knew that the scourge would soon be with them, especially when the motherships made space fall close to Earth.

She stood and screamed to the heavens, "What do you want from us? Why are you doing this?!"

Joe stood and wrapped Andie in his arms from behind. "Shh," he whispered. "It's okay. We're going to find a way to make it."

Andie pulled abruptly away. "Don't!" she with said angry tears on her cheeks. "Don't tell me stories. We are going to fight. We are going to survive!"

She bent over and gasped deep breaths. "Damn the spaceships and the frakkin' aliens! Come and get us, you alien bastards!"

From inside the cabin, Satchmo made a soft bark. Andie looked up at Joe and said with a sharp edge to her voice, "I'm done with the radio. No more. Got it?"

Joe nodded, picked up the solar radio and placed into the back of the Rav 4. He followed Andie into the cabin, closing and latching the door as the sun set on a threatened planet.

# CHAPTER 20

The days passed, one grueling day after another, with both Andie and Joe laboring to ensure their survival. Andie had begun weaving sisal rope with twigs and small branches and nailing each length to the cabin's roof. She planned on weaving more brush between the hanging ropes so that the ultimate effect would look more natural and wild. Joe focused on fishing for part of each day and caught trout under the low hanging branches in eddies across the stream. He was disappointed that he had forgotten to pick up a net to scoop the fish out of the water. He managed to save most of his catches, and they took turns frying the fish in a pan with oil and some herbs for flavoring.

It was clear to both Andie and Joe that their food supply was not going to last as long as they had envisioned. Their physical labors created a ravenous hunger at the end of a day, and they ate more canned fruits and vegetables to meet their appetites. They had discussed that once the planetary ships arrived, they probably wouldn't be able to be outdoors as much, nor would they be able to cook and have smoke appearing above their chimney.

Satchmo healed a little more each day, and he, too, was hungry after having a limited appetite from his surgery and the first week of convalescence. He wasn't totally back to his fighting weight, but it wouldn't be long before he was the stocky fellow he had been.

All of these potential problems caused Joe to consider their situation, and he shared his thoughts with Andie. He had to take action while there was still time. Andie knew that he listened to his solar radio while she was at the stream bathing. He'd tuned in to the same station that had given them information and caught one broadcast the day before. Although he risked upsetting her, he told her that the alien motherships were still on course for Earth, and new calculations had predicted that it would be maybe a week before arrival. She was gratified that, as in world crises before, different nations around the world were working together to create a solid resistance with all available weaponry. The major obstacle to complete obliteration of the ships was the need to keep the human race alive. Nuclear weapons would probably work against the aliens, but they would have to be a last resort. Lasers and sound wave particle attacks were a part of the arsenal, but their effectiveness couldn't be determined until the aliens were in their atmosphere.

Andie found it amusing that a small group of people believed that the mother ships were coming to bring peace to the world, and that the initial assault by the discs had been a mistake. These pro-alien groups gathered to think of ways that they could greet the aliens that would show that the human race was good and welcoming. 'Yeah,' Andie thought. 'Good luck with that.'

Andie was not naïve, and she knew that Joe was still keeping tabs on the news. She was aware that knowledge was a tool in their own arsenal, and that they needed to be as prepared as they could be, in their sanctuary in the woods. 'Forewarned is forearmed,' she said her herself. But she still couldn't handle the stress of hearing the dire news on a regular basis. She and Joe had been through so much, Satchmo included, and she needed time to regroup and clear her thoughts. There was no doubt that more, and probably worse, was coming their way. She would face it when she had to, of that she was certain.

Joe walked over to stand beside Andie. "Hey, that's looking good," he said, admiring her handiwork with the hanging ropes.

"Thanks," Andie replied, wiping sweat out of her eyes with the back of her hand. The weather was getting warmer as they approached the month of June. "But I'm worried that there won't be enough of the sisal to finish the covering." She stood back and appraised her work.

"I was wondering about that. And other things, too," Joe said.

"Oh?" Andie said as her gaze met his glance.

"Andie, there's a bunch of stuff we need, like more food, netting, water jugs, rope. I think I'm going to go back into town and resupply." He toed the dirt under his shoe.

"Joe, that's too risky, and you know it!" Andie suddenly felt chilled to her core. "What if the aliens come, and you're not here? What if they're in the town or up on the highway?"

"Andie, I don't think we have a choice. Our supplies look okay for now, but we need to have enough to get us through the long haul. We don't know how many months or years the invasion is going to last. I'm sure these aliens aren't just going to keel over and die from our viruses or the common cold. We need to be prepared."

"We've been working hard," Andie said.

"We've done alright, Andie," Joe said. "But we need to grab this window of opportunity to get even more."

Andie stared at his tanned handsome face, with the mustache and beard that were steadily growing and covering his handsome features. "Joe…"

"Andie, I'll come back. I promise," he said. Then he grinned. "I'll bring you back a Coke."

Andie had to smile at his offer. He was learning her weaknesses all too well.

"You'll have to fix the driveway when you get back," she reminded him in one last attempt to stop him from leaving.

"This time you're going to help me, right?" he asked, somehow flirting and wheedling at the same time.

"You bring me that Coke, and you're on," she said. She tilted her head in her own flirty, challenging way.

"I'll go tomorrow morning early, before the crow," Joe stated.

"I'll see if I can think of anything else we need," she offered. "I'll go make a list." She went inside the cabin, much to Satchmo's delight. He preferred the company of his humans than lying alone on his bed.

"That's my Andie," Joe said. He followed her into the cabin to spend some time with Satchmo. "I sure hope the camping store still has some things we can use. But I especially hope that they have a big, 'ole bag of dog biscuits for you, buddy." He rubbed Satchmo's ears and kissed him on the cold, wet nose.

The next morning Joe was sent on his way with a wave from Andie and a bark from Satchmo. It was a little rough going as the Rav 4 climbed over the grasses and brush on the driveway, but soon the car gained enough traction to send it onto Skyline Drive.

Andie decided to work for awhile on the camouflage ropes and soon finished with the last bit of sisal within the hour. The cabin was only half covered, including the front and the side with the window. When viewed while standing several feet away from these two sides, the cabin looked rather magical and ethereal. Andie picked up Joe's fishing rod from inside the cabin, gave Satch a petting and then walked down to the waterfront. She carried the water bucket to put any fish in should she get lucky with the fishing. For the time being, she turned it upside down and used it as a seat as she baited the hook with a worm she had just dug up with a spoon. She was surprised that she wasn't squeamish in the least with the whole process of fishing. Not to mention, she was pretty handy at filleting a fish. She would love to surprise Joe with some fresh fish for dinner this evening.

She cast the line across the stream and reeled the filament back towards her. After casting several times with no nibbles, she felt the line tug. She had a bite, maybe even a fish on the hook. She continued reeling in the line so as not to cause a jerk which might make her lose the catch. Sure enough, there was a large shiny-scaled fish wiggling on the end of her rod. Holding the rod in one hand, she overturned the bucket and dipped it into the stream to fill it partially with the cool spring water. She then released the fish from the hook and watched as it plopped into the bucket. Andie did a short happy dance then began to cast her rod again. One large fish was good, two large fish would be even better.

She considered how she would prepare the fish using a coating of breadcrumbs. She'd use the last of the stale bread she had and bake it over a fire before crumbling it into tiny pieces. They had rigged a foil pan attached to two sticks which they positioned over a small fire pit. It was primitive, but effective. The shortening they had might work to make the coating stick to the fish. Andie smiled to herself. If only the television chefs could see her now. Forget teaching high school students. She would become famous showing people how to cook in the woods with only the bare essentials.

Andie heard a sound and whipped her head towards the cabin. A black bear was loping towards the cabin, sniffing at the various pieces of twigs and vines on the sisal ropes. Andie held her breath, frozen in place at the shock of seeing such a large creature in the wild. And so close to her. Perhaps if she stayed quiet and still it would walk back into the woods where it belonged. But her wish was denied as the bear stood up on two legs and began pawing at the sisal ropes. To make things worse, Satchmo had smelled the bear and began growling to ward it away. The bear, instead of being frightened by Satch's growls, began to move and reached in towards the cabin. Satch was at the front door, and the front door was closed but not latched. If the bear discovered this and pushed on the door, Satch would soon be lunch.

Andie frantically looked around her for a weapon, or something to distract the bear from the cabin and the barking dog inside. She looked down at the fish in the bucket, and without hesitation, picked up the fish with her bare hands. She pulled back her arm and sent the fish flying towards the cabin but away from the door. The bear fell down to its haunches and ran over to the fish. Satchmo had stopped barking, but now Andie saw that she had created a new problem. After the bear had devoured the fish, he would undoubtably look around for more. At the water. Where Andie was standing.

She put down the fishing rod and walked into the water. She hoped that the roaring stream would mask her scent so that the bear wouldn't find her. She walked in deeper and shivered at the chill of the water. There was nothing else she could do except maybe get to the other shore and hide out of sight. The bear had indeed turned and looked towards her.

Andie remembered that Joe had said that there were a series of rocks that looked like stepping stones near the middle of the stream. She continued further in the water, which got progressively deeper and more difficult to traverse as the current headed downstream. Finding one of the rocks, she pulled herself up on to it and tried to stand. But the green lichen on the rock proved slippery and wet, and she fell into the stream sideways with her head sinking under the water. Andie pushed up and held on to a jagged rock, gasping for air. She looked towards the shore and saw the bear smelling the fishing rod and nosing it into the water. Purposely going underwater again, she hoped that she was washing away any traces of her own smell and that of the fish she had caught.

The black bear took a long drink at the water's edge, then turned and lumbered back into the woods. Andie didn't have the strength to feel relief. She was chilled from head to toe, and she was starting to notice a dull pain in the front of her left leg. She tried to stand, but immediately flopped back down into the water, with water cascading over head and shoulders. She had to get out of the water, and soon. She wasn't sure if her leg was bleeding but she felt that it was a strong possibility.

Again, she lifted herself up from the bottom of the stream and turned over on to her stomach. Inch by inch she pulled herself to rocks and crevices where she could get a handhold. She almost got to the water's edge when she collapsed with exhaustion. She knew she was in shock from the cold water and her injury. Her breathing was labored as she tried to stay focused. 'One more try,' she told herself. 'I can do this. One more try.'

And with one more attempt to crawl out of the stream, Andie made it to the shore. She lay for a few minutes, letting the sun warm and comfort her. She sat up and looked down at her legs and discovered a three-inch tear in her left leg. It was steadily bleeding. Andie ripped off her shirt and wound it tightly around her leg to staunch the bleeding. She had to get into the cabin for the bandages and first aid kit. So, she crawled on her hands and knees across the yard. The pain from her leg was intense, but endorphins from her ordeal with the black bear gave her the extra push she needed to get to safety.

She crashed into the cabin's door, and Satch ran towards her, licking her face and wagging his tail. It was as if he knew what she had done to save him. Andie sank flat down on her stomach, her head resting on the wood floor. She decided to rest stay there for a few more minutes. It was so nice on the floor. Very, very nice.

# *CHAPTER 21*

Andie woke up screaming. Someone was pinning her down on the floor, and she couldn't move. She tried to squirm away, but then heard the one voice that could make this right.

"Andie! Please lay back down. I'm trying to fix your leg," Joe said.

Andie rolled on to her back and gazed up into Joe's eyes. "I thought you were a bear."

"Hold that thought," he said then released his hold on her.

Joe searched the cabin for the bucket, but couldn't find it. He ran outside to the car and grabbed a new one he'd obtained in town. Then he ran to the creek and filled it halfway with water. Satchmo stood at the open cabin door and watched his owner sprint back to the cabin. "Look out, Satch. I'm coming back in," Joe called. He grabbed a few pieces of clothing that looked clean, and drenched them with the water. Then he gently wiped down Andie's legs to remove dried blood and any debris in the wound. He took the peroxide out of the First Aid kit, his hands shaking with nervousness. He looked at Andie's peaceful face, and said a quiet prayer. "I'm sorry, Andie. This is going to hurt. Bad." He placed a pile of cloths under her leg to catch the overflow of liquid, then carefully poured the peroxide into the wound.

"It hurts, it hurts," she moaned. "Oh, my God!"

"I know, but that just means its working, all right? It should start feeling better in a few minutes." Andie's face was as white as the sheet she was lying on.

Joe rinsed and gently wiped the peroxide from the wound. "It's not as deep as I thought it was. There was a lot of blood but it stopped on its own while you were dozing." He applied antibiotic ointment to the wound and then put a large padded bandage on the area using medical tape.

"Joe, there was a bear, right here at the cabin. He tried to get Satchmo. The darn dog kept barking, I was fishing, and so I threw this large fish I caught across the yard to distract the bear. And it worked. And Satch stopped barking. But then the bear saw me and the only thing I could think of to do was to get into the water and sort of hide there. I fell on the rocks, and the water kept pouring over me. But the bear didn't come into the water. He just walked back into the woods."

Joe shook his head in disbelief. "And you were afraid I was going to get hurt in town. We never imagined that something could happen here."

"I know," Andie said. "I never imagined…"

"It's my fault," said Joe. "I should have left the gun with you."

"No, I wouldn't have known how to use it," Andie said.

"I'll teach you, Andie." Joe rubbed her arm. "I didn't see any major swelling except near the cut. You don't think you broke anything, do you?"

Andie shook her head, "I don't think so, but I did fall when I tried to stand on the bank of the stream after the bear went away."

"You were probably just woozy. I guess we won't know until you get some rest. We can check it out tomorrow. For now, I'm going to give you something to help with the pain. I bet you're going to be black and blue tomorrow."

Joe helped Andie sit on the bed, and she sucked down the pills with a mug of water. She closed her eyes and breathed a sigh. "I'm so glad you're back, Joe."

Joe laughed. "You should have seen my heroic return. I walked into the cabin, all excited to show you my bounty, and there you were lying on the floor. But, hey, you'll be even more glad when you see all the loot I found in town. Why don't you rest a while and I'll start emptying the car."

"Okay," she agreed.

Andie and Satch watched Joe as he came into and out of the cabin. He unloaded the car and placed piles of paper goods, utensils, blankets, rope, and dozens of food cans of every sort in every available space. It was a total mess, and Andie knew she'd be reorganizing everything once she felt better. Joe started a small fire in the fireplace and put on a pot of hot dogs and beans to heat. He drove the car around the cabin to the side furthest from the driveway. And then he filled his bucket of water to wash Andie's blood trail through the grass. Andie watched him through the open cabin door and realized that Joe felt the blood might draw other animals to their site. The bear might even return if it got hungry enough, but it was spring and so that was highly unlikely with all the berries and roots available in the woods.

"So, now we have aliens, wild animals and criminals after us." He dished up the dinner into bowls and placed them on the table. As Andie hobbled over, with Satchmo in her way at every step, Joe looked up the driveway, noting his car tracks in the weeds.

"I'll cover the car tracks tomorrow. I'm tired and hungry, so let's dig in!" Joe said as he held out a chair for Andie.

She smiled at him and took her seat. As she looked around the room, taking in the stores of food and supplies, the bulldog at her feet, and the man across the table from her, she felt comfort and hope. It was enough for now.

# *CHAPTER 22*

"Joe," Andie said.

"Yes?" Joe replied. He was lying right next to her on the bed, ever so careful not to move and cause Andie any pain. It was hard to do, considering that she was bruised over half her body. He'd been sleeping on the floor in his sleeping bag but had joined Andie on the bed at her request when she awoke.

"My leg isn't broken. I probably just twisted it when I fell onto the rocks. And I can move it side to side now," Andie said.

"Mmm-hmm," he replied. They had been having this same conversation since yesterday, and it always ended the same…with Andie claiming she was fine and that she should be allowed out of the cabin.

"Andie, you know how I feel about this," Joe said. "Yes, I know you didn't break your leg, but you're still unsteady. and I don't want you tripping over some rock and breaking your neck."

Andie sighed deeply. "I'm getting bored and frustrated."

"I'd rather have you bored than injured because you got up too soon." He turned on his side to face her. "I have some of that reusable stretch bandage that we can wrap around your leg. It would support you and keep you from overdoing things.'

"That could work," Andie stuck out her chin and pursed her lips as she considered the idea. "Let's do it."

"Give me one more day, and then we'll try it out."

"Another day? We really don't have that much time to play around with," she noted. "I mean, imminent threat of super-sized alien spaceships coming our way, remember?"

"I think we have to do what's right for you." Joe reached over and tucked a loose strand of hair behind her ear.

"Joe, you should start sleeping in the bed again. It's big enough, and the floor has got to be uncomfortable, even with the two sleeping bags," Andie said.

"I'm doing fine. I can certainly stand another night cuddling with Satch."

Andie laughed. Satch had taken Joe's temporary sleeping arrangement as an invitation to share body warmth. "He'll miss you when you return to the bed."

Joe's face lifted in a smile of acknowledgment. "I'm just glad that I managed to get all of the supplies when I went into town. Especially, the portable toilet."

"That will save us a ton of embarrassment, although I still feel weird about you monitoring my every move." Andie pinched her eyes closed and tried to forget how she caught Joe watching her as she struggled with dressing.

"No sweat, Andie," Joe answered.

"And I can't believe how much canned food June gave you." Joe had stopped by the restaurant to check in on June during his foraging expedition. June was doing fine, although she still hadn't heard from her husband, Dan.

"Yeah, well, I hope you like canned baked beans because we have enough to feed an army. Those cans are huge."

"I just wish she had come back with you. I can't help but think about her working at the restaurant and waiting for her husband to come home," Andie said.

"I know. I feel the same way. It would be a miracle if he could make it, driving a tractor-trailer through all those large cities. I told June she could leave a note for him on one of the tables in the restaurant, but she just wasn't budging." Joe pushed his head deeper into the pillow. "I respect her choice, but I'm not sure it's the right one."

"Thank heavens the aliens haven't infiltrated the town yet. Maybe they never will. Maybe its small potatoes for them."

"For now," Joe said.

"Do you know something I don't?"

"Not really, but I have been wondering why the alien bastards are here in the first place. Are they just a nasty, vindictive lot who want to destroy us just because we are in control of a planet? Or do they want to take over Earth for themselves? Why do they have to hunt us?"

"Yeah! What have we done to make them destroy us?" Andie said.

"What have we done…"

"We've done nothing."

Joe laid still for a few moments, his brow furrowed. "That may be true. Or maybe we have done something but we just don't understand what that is."

"Oy, that's getting too vague for me," Andie said. "But I do think about how people have said that we may have descended from an alien species that landed here on Earth."

"And what? They now want to do away with their human offspring after all these millennia?" Joe said. "That's a kick in the genetics."

"I didn't say that, per se. But maybe there is something the aliens have come back for, and we're standing in their way."

"And, as you always say, why just us, and not the animals?"

"Maybe they'll let some of us live. But I kind of doubt that given their track record. We have to continue to do everything we can to ensure our survival."

"And then some," Joe said. "I hid the car in the woods and covered it with all sorts of branches and bushes. I don't want anything around here that spells out 'human.'"

"And you covered the driveway again."

"Yes, I did. I worked on some of your camouflage for the cabin, too."

"Maybe we, and by we I mean you, can bring in some stuff tomorrow so I can work on it while I rest my leg. What do you think?" Andie asked.

"Can do."

"Are they getting much closer, Joe?"

"Yes, pretty soon we'll be able to see them with our naked eyes."

Andie nodded. "Okay. Game on. Now how about some of those beans for lunch? I'm as hungry as a bear."

"And you would know how hungry a bear gets," Joe said.

"Not very funny, Joe."

He smiled at her as he slid off the bed. "Beans, the meal that keeps on giving."

Andie just shook her head at his antics. "Speak for yourself. I'm a lady."

The next day meant more of the same – working to fortify their shelter. Joe spent most of his time outdoors, placing more brush and plant roots on the roof and hanging the sisal rope camouflage that Andie was making indoors. She sat at their small table by the window, leaving the glass uncovered to give her more light to work by. Her injured leg was supported by the other kitchen chair. Joe hadn't fashioned a brace for it yet. But she knew it was only a matter of time. Joe was a man of his word, and industrious as well. Most of her family and friends held white-collar jobs in business, retail or education. They didn't have to work with their hands, except for gardening or keeping the lawn trimmed. She was working harder than she ever had, even with her past years teaching feisty adolescents. Kids sure kept her running, but it didn't involve constant contact with nature. Dirt that got under the fingernails wasn't something she was used to.

Andie wove the loose branches, some with new green leaves, on to the rope. She was enjoying the process, even though Joe had to be the one to hang the finished vines. She was optimistic about the healing of her leg wound and was anxious to go fishing again. Some nice fresh fish would taste so good. Maybe she could ask Joe to try for some trout this afternoon.

She completed a length of rope and held it up to the light. Then she put it carefully on the floor and took a deep gulp of water. How easy it was to get used to this way of living, wild and free in the woods. She had always loved travelling and pushing herself to explore new places. The Caribbean Islands were her top destinations with hot sand, warm ocean water and a world of sea creatures to watch. When the aliens left, she would one day go back to Belize or Jamaica. Andie shook her head, as if to erase such thoughts. She knew these were daydreams, and life had become so much harder. She might never get back to the islands. Or even to her home in Columbia, for that matter.

She thought about her hometown and all the people and stores she knew there. She loved living in Columbia with everything she needed just a few minutes from her apartment. Sure, it was a busy place with heavy traffic on the roads. But the parks and walking trails more than made up for the bustle of her suburban home. How were people surviving with those alien discs around every corner? Her own brother lived close to Boston, and so he, too, was in the same situation she had been in. Where did he get his food? People were going to run out of supplies, and then what? Andie felt her heart beating faster as she considered the horrors that people were facing. The discs went where most people resided. They weren't here in the woods or mountains. They were terrorizing the cities. People had to stay inside to maintain a modicum of safety. It was as if they were being herded. The aliens weren't going indoors, they were just policing the outdoors. But people couldn't stay inside forever. Especially now that the large mother ships were approaching.

Andie picked up another length of rope and began her work again. She had to face it. Not many people were going to survive this. Who knows what the larger ships would bring, but it wasn't going to be anything good for mankind. She and Joe might make it, but would they want to live in a world where aliens were constantly seeking them out? So many questions, and no answers. Andie knew she would have to keep her emotions on an even keel, if she had any hope of fighting the unknown. She needed to stay sharp for Joe, and for Satchmo. No more accidents, she admonished herself.

At that moment Satchmo grumbled in his sleep, and Andie smiled to hear such an ordinary noise. Satchmo was content to be wherever Joe was. They were bonded for life. And she was just someone who happened to stumble across their paths. It had been her lucky day when she met the two.

Suddenly, Satch shot up and ran to the door barking as if he were being attacked.

Andie stood up and ran over to Satch.

"Andie! Stay inside!" Joe called from somewhere in front of the building.

That's when she heard the deep growling. It was the bear. It had returned.

She reached down to grab Satch's collar and pull him away from the door. She managed to get to the bed, where she plopped down and then pulled the trembling dog up on to her lap. "Shh. Satch. Quiet." She stroked the fur on his head and back and tried to impart calm. "That's it. Good boy."

She then heard a repeated popping sound. Joe had fired upon the bear until there were no more bullets in the gun. She closed her eyes and prayed for Joe and for the bear. She hoped the bear wouldn't suffer but she also knew Joe had used the gun as a last resort.

The cabin door opened slowly, and Joe entered, white-faced and drawing deep breaths.

"It's okay. I got him," he said. "Hey, we got any more of those Cokes?"

# CHAPTER 23

The day went by quickly once Joe got over his shock. He was kept busy with moving the bear away from the cabin site, using the once-again uncovered Rav 4 to push the heavy beast into the rushing stream. The water didn't carry the bear away, but it certainly covered its scent from other predators. Fortunately, Joe was able to position the bear far downstream so that any water they used wouldn't be contaminated by the eventually decaying body. Andie nervously hung around the open doorway with Satch, praying that the Rav wouldn't end up in the water with the bear. Satchmo was overexcited from all the noise and activity; he was practically prancing in the grass. The bulldog was certainly feeling much better with only a slight limp with his back leg. Andie tested out her own leg, putting more weight on it and swinging it in different directions to test her range of motion. She was ready to get outdoors.

When Joe finally returned to the cabin, slick with the sweat from his efforts and from the warming afternoon, he sank into a chair and shook his head. "If it's not one thing, it's another," he said.

Andie pulled a Coke from the cabinet and handed it to him. "You've earned this one, too."

Joe took the can, popped the top and drank the soda in one continuous gulp. "We're going through this soda fast, but the commercials were right. It's the real thing."

"Joe…" began Andie. But he held up his hand to stop her. Joe stood, opened his mouth wide and gave a long, loud burp.

"That's what I'm talking about," he said, satisfied. "Now you were saying?"

Andie laughed and gave him a wide smile. "I don't remember. Wait. I do! Please wrap my leg. That's the last thing you need to do for today. I promise."

Joe gave her a sideways glance. "Is that right? The only thing, besides covering up the Rav again and making sure there isn't a bloody patch where the bear fell?"

"Oh. Well, yes, after those things." She bit her lip, and drew in a deep breath. "I have to get out of this cabin. You've heard of cabin fever, right? Well, I have it bad. I'm trying to be patient, but I just want to get up and out. I think if you tape my leg, then I can get back to doing things. Like sweeping out this cabin. All those twigs and leaves and dog hair- I can get rid of them all."

"Andie, girl, I was just teasing you. Honestly. And just having you here has been so good. We're doing this together."

Joe gathered the bandages he needed to bind her leg, and soon she had a wrapping that let her walk and yet gave her support. Promising Joe not to overdo it, she grabbed the broom and soon swept the debris, and Satchmo, out the door and into the fresh spring day. She sat down on the folding chair next to the solar radio and sighed in satisfaction. She could hear Joe tossing branches onto the car to cover it from any malevolent eyes. In the daylight, she could only see the blue skies and the scudding clouds above, but she knew in her heart that the day was soon coming when the skies would be filled with extraterrestrial invaders.

She had asked Joe to listen to the radio when she wasn't around to hear it. She had wanted to remain oblivious to any painful news. But she knew in her heart that putting her head in the sand was just a stopgap measure. The aliens were coming whether she paid attention to them or not. She needed to be informed in order to help herself and the others.

Andie turned the knob on the radio and made certain that the usual radio station was locked on. She listened to some static, but then found a station that was sending out a signal.

"With what information we have gathered from NOAA, the National Oceanic and Atmospheric Administration, and various international weather stations, it appears that the enemy convoy is within range of our solar system and will make contact with our atmosphere in two days. We do not know the intentions of the invaders, but the killing machines that are already here have shown us that we had better prepare for the worst. Get to a safe place. Try to get out of the cities, away from high population centers. We know that if a black, disc-shaped object comes close, you must freeze your body until the machine is out of sight. So, there are ways to escape, although it is very difficult. For those who plan on sheltering in place, try to collect food and medical supplies. Officials don't know how long the presumed assault will be or what form it will take. But we do know, our government will fight back.

We expect a hard and sustained battle, using all the weapons in our arsenal, to defend our territory and our people. Many people will not survive. That is a given, unfortunately. But, just maybe, humankind will continue and regain our place in the universe. This is Station KCMO out of Missouri, signing off for now. God Bless."

Andie turned off the radio and sat staring into her surroundings. Wildflowers were just beginning to show, with their purple and yellow crests, by the riverbank. Blue jays and robins darted among the tree branches, with the soft green leaves. It was a lovely day. And the day after tomorrow, it might be the beginning of the end. She turned around to look at the cabin, adorned in branches and weeds and grass. Would it fool an alien into thinking it was not a home, inhabited by humans? She wasn't sure. They couldn't even fool a bear, let alone an intelligent species.

Then she had a sobering thought. Maybe they should leave. They could go further up into the mountains that were in the distance. They hadn't really explored the area. They had just stopped when they got to the cabin. They were sitting ducks down here in the little valley by the water.

Satchmo walked over to her and whomped his body down at her feet. He looked up at her with his deep brown trusting eyes. "Shit, Satch. Don't look at me like that." Her thoughts drifted to her loved ones, her family, her friends, her students. She hadn't done anything to protect the ones she loved. She had run away to the mountains like a coward, and for what? To protect herself, with a guy she hardly knew and an old wrinkled dog. She felt pathetic.

But then, she looked at Satch again, and felt the trust and love radiating from his warm little body. She bent down and rubbed the back of his neck where he liked it best. "Satch, you're the good boy. You're the best boy." Just touching him made her feel calmer. Satch had saved them, and she had done her best to save him. It had to be good enough. It had to count. In a world gone crazy, it came down to the little things and the little connections. She and Joe had a connection, too. Even if it was based on survival and not love, what they had was enough to carry them through to whatever came next.

She would worry about the rest of the world another time. Right now, it was all about the three of them. If she thought too much about the big picture, she would surely lose her mind. So, she stood and walked into the cabin to make dinner. Beans and maybe canned fruit. That would taste good. She could see Joe walking towards the open grassy area where the bear had been shot. Too bad they had both been queasy about obtaining and eating bear meat. That day might come, but not today.

# *CHAPTER 24*

Another two days melted away as Andie and Joe kept themselves busy with organizing their stores of food and emergency supplies. Joe caught several fish and cooked them over an open fire. It smelled so good that their mouths were watering along with Satchmo's. They ate their feast with canned corn and some packaged mashed potatoes. Every once in a while, they'd check the skies, but in the day light there was still nothing to see. However, on the second night, there could be no denying it. The alien ships could be seen at dusk, and only grew bigger in the passing hours.

Joe and Andie sat with Satchmo on the ground outside the door of their cabin. As the motherships grew impossibly larger, with illuminated areas along the sides, Andie began to feel a sense of déjà vu. She wrapped her arms around herself, and whispered, "Oh, God. This is it.

This is the dream I've been having since childhood."

Joe moved closer to Andie and said, "Tell me about it."

"In the dream, I was always standing looking up at the night sky. Then weirdly, the stars started to coalesce. It was like they were dancing in a pattern. And then, as the stars started to fall closer to Earth, I realized that they were spaceships, and that they were coming to land."

"Did you sense that they were evil?" Joe asked.

"Yes," Andie answered. "I had a second dream about the aliens where they were in small spaceships that moved slowly past buildings, searching for people. They had a laser device that they could shine in windows to detect the presence of people. The laser made a humming noise, and its light would sweep across a room. I always would slide out of bed to the floor on the side away from the window. I was never caught. But it scared the hell out of me both in the dream and in real life when I woke up."

"Nightmares," Joe said.

"That are coming to life," said Andie watched as the mother ships spread out and headed in different directions. The motherships seemed graceful for their size. One ship headed towards them, and as it drew closer, it made an incredible roaring sound. The winds whipped, and the trees in Shenandoah began to bend and shake, as if in the winds of a hurricane.

"Let's get inside!" Joe shouted. He helped Andie crawl into the cabin, and he shut the door with a bang.

"Dear heavens," Andie said as she cuddled Satchmo.

"That one ship is about a mile away, and it looks like it's right on top of us. I bet it's here because of Washington, D.C. The other ships may have gone to other major cities in any country,"

"On any continent," Andie added.

"Right," said Joe. "They're as big as a major city. How many aliens could be inside?"

"When I was young, despite my scary dreams, I wanted aliens to come to Earth. I wanted to meet them and learn more about our universe. I wanted to travel to the stars and planets. I romanticized the contact with aliens." Andie sighed. "This is not what I envisioned."

"Most of the science fiction books I read had the aliens as aggressors. Same with the movies, except for the one with the close encounters," Joe commented.

"I doubt there will be musical scales coming from those ships. And I guess we'll find out if there any little green aliens on board."

"I just can't see little green men as the instigators of an alien invasion. Now if they look like the creatures from War of the Worlds, that might make more sense." Joe cocked an eye towards Andie.

Andie shuddered. "I don't think I'm going to be able to sleep tonight, and your bedtime stories aren't helping me to calm down."

"Sorry. I guess I let my mouth run when I get nervous. Let's get to bed and try to relax. We'll take things as they come."

Andie slid into the bed and, to Joe's surprise, she wrapped her arms around his chest when he settled in next to her. Neither could sleep as their cabin window pulsed with the light from the mothership, even with the heavy curtains closed.

# *CHAPTER 25*

"What was that noise?" Andie asked, frightened by the crashing sound she'd heard. Joe was already up and out of bed, heading for the door. He unlatched it and peered outside.

"I don't see anything," he whispered. "It sounded further away, like up on the drive. Let's get dressed and check it out." He didn't have to say anything else, as Andie had already grabbed a pair of jeans and a tee shirt. She wasn't even concerned with Joe catching sight of her underwear.

Satchmo jumped up at Joe's legs, showing his eagerness to go outside with his friends, but Joe gently pushed him down. "No, Satch, stay here." Satch looked sad, but quietly loped to his sleeping area. "Good boy," Joe said.

Andie and Joe slipped out the doorway, latching the external lock for Satch's protection. They walked through the spring grasses and headed up the gravel driveway, now hidden beneath every loose branch and stone Joe could find. As they reached the top of the driveway, just a few feet from Skyline Drive, Joe put his finger to his lips to remind Andie to remain silent. He then placed himself behind a wide tree trunk and gestured Andie to do the same. They peered in each direction but saw nothing out of the ordinary. Joe shrugged his shoulders and was about to walk the remaining feet to the Skyline Drive when suddenly a car burst out of the tunnel in the distance to their right. It screeched as it's driver almost lost control of the sedan on the curb. Then the driver regained control and headed towards Joe and Andie at breakneck speed. With only seconds left before the car passed them by, another sound came crashing out of the tunnel. It was a contraption unlike any human had seen before, and it was tracking the speeding car. The metallic-like gold machine was built like a tripod, with wheels instead of feet. It stood about ten feet tall, and had a spheroid attachment at the top of its long body. The attachment irised open and a red, pulsing light beamed forward.

"Down!" Joe whispered and pushed Andie face first into the dirt beneath her tree. She found it hard to breathe and couldn't move due to the fear that held her frozen in place. Just then, they heard the sharp sound as a laser pierced the air. They heard the explosion and felt its heat for a brief moment as the car was destroyed. Small pieces of the car rained down on the road and into the forest.

The alien machine continued rolling down the Drive without stopping to inspect the destruction it had caused. Andie could hear its wheels on the pavement and didn't raise her head until she could no longer hear the foreign sound of the construct on pavement.

"Okay," Joe whispered. Andie lifted her head, wiping dirt and dead leaves from her face and clothing. She scanned the road in front of her and saw only small remnants of the car, and nothing of the people who may have been in it. "Oh my God."

"Those aliens aren't playing around if they're sending those robots out into the countryside," Joe said as he continued to gaze in the direction the tripod had gone.

"Yes," Andie agreed in a shaky voice. "But it seems like those things wouldn't do too well in the woods or on a mountain with those wheels."

As she finished her sentence, she heard another sound coming from the end of the tunnel. "Oh, no," she moaned. "What next?"

But this time, the car they spotted at the end of the tunnel stopped and several people got out and ran into the woods. Andie turned to Joe, "Friend or foe, do you think?"

"Not sure. But they were smart to ditch their car. They at least have a chance if they hide in the woods."

"Like us."

"Yes, like us," Joe said. "Let's get back to the cabin. We're probably safer there than anywhere else right now."

"I'm not sure of that. I think we really need to consider moving further into the mountains." Andie continued to feel that this would be a better option. The look on Joe's face told her that he wasn't going to change his mind, at least not at that moment.

"Okay, let's go back. I'm hungry." She turned and headed back down the driveway, picking her way over and through the scattered brush. She didn't wait to see if Joe was behind her. She was starting to work up an anger at him, for his unwillingness to move from their camp site.

As she clomped through the grass, as a show of defiance if Joe was watching, she realized the door of the cabin was ajar. She cautiously walked to the cabin and peeked inside. Nothing unusual.

She breathed a sigh of relief and pulled the door open further. That's when she noticed that there was no dog to welcome her. "Satch?" she called.

Joe had just reached her side and looked at her. "What?"

"Joe, Satch is gone! I know we locked the outside latch when we left. How did he get out?"

Joe's face drained of color, and he began to run across the yard to the right side of the woods. "Satch!" he called. Andie ran to the other side of the woods, and called out, "Here, boy. Come on, Satch." Neither person received a bark in reply or a rustle among the bushes. They each went into the woods further than they had before, and further than was wise, considering the potential alien threat. After several minutes they met at the bank of the stream. Joe's face looked bleak and worried. "He can't take care of himself if he's lost."

Andie hooked her hand around Joe's upper arm, and said, "He'll be okay. He'll come back. You know he will."

Then, before they could fully turn, they heard a loud scraping sound coming from the woods behind the cabin. Two young men stepped out into the open, one cradling Satchmo in his arms.

"Hey, is this guy yours?" one of the men called out with a smile.

Satchmo gave a soft bark, then wiggled in the man's arms so that he could lick his face.

"Crisis averted," Andie muttered. "Stupid dog, you scared us half to death."

# *CHAPTER 26*

Satchmo slid down from the man's arms and ran over to Joe. Joe knelt down and rubbed Satchmo's ears. "Hey, buddy. Where were you, huh?"

Satchmo gave a little dance, twerking his bottom and shaking his bobbed tail.

"I guess we need to apologize," the young man with hair to his shoulders and bright blue eyes offered. "We were crossing the stream and saw your, um, home? So, we knocked, but no one answered. I lifted the latch and pulled the door open a hair, and that dog just shot out before we knew what was happening."

The other man, with soft blue eyes, shorter hair and a green camp shirt, continued. "We saw that no one was in the cabin, so we chased after him. He ran behind the cabin, by your covered car, good job by the way, and relieved himself. We easily got hold of him then."

Joe stood and nodded. "Well, thanks for corralling him. He can be feisty."

Andie commented, "Ha! You don't know the half of it. Listen, why don't we go into the cabin. I feel exposed out here, especially after seeing that tripod monster on the road." She pulled open the door, and the foursome trooped in, with Satchmo weaving among the legs like ribbons on a Maypole.

"Did you see the rolling tripod?" Joe asked the men as he gestured for them to sit in the available chairs. As the men dumped backpacks and gear onto the floor, Andie plopped on to the bed. Joe came over and sat on the floor at her feet.

"God, yes," said the longer-haired man. "That's why we jumped out of our car and abandoned it at the end of the tunnel about a half mile from here."

"We saw you," said Andie. "You're lucky the tripod was so focused on the car that was ahead of you. "

"Yes, or otherwise we would have been blasted to smithereens instead of sitting in this cabin with you. By the way, I'm Phil," the guy with the shorter hair said. He stood up and walked over to shake hands with Joe and Andie.

"And I'm Pat," the other man followed suit and shook hands as well.

"And we're Andie and Joe," Andie offered.

As the men walked back to their chairs, Andie said. "So you guys are either twins, or one of you has been cloned by the aliens."

Pat laughed. "Good one. I'll have to remember that if the aliens don't destroy all of humanity in the next few days."

"Where are you from, and even more importantly, where are you going?" Joe asked. "You're welcome to bunker down with us, if it suits you. It's not fancy, but it's kept us safe for the last week. And we have lots of canned goods."

"Well, that's a nice offer, but we decided we want to go higher ground," Pat replied.

Phil nodded his head, and then said, "We lived in Adams Morgan, in Washington, until we realized that the shit was hitting the fan, and we were pretty much sitting ducks in our townhouse. It was hard going, with those freaking ETs all over the place."

"They're killing machines," Andie said. "They got a friend of mine."

Pat nodded sympathetically. "I'm sorry. The machines got a lot of people, but they were inefficient if they were meant to get everyone. They could only identify us when we were moving. Hey, I can play statues as good as the next kid."

Joe chimed in, "Yeah, but now we have the rolling tripods that seem to go after moving cars as well. Maybe their programming indicates that they know that only people drive vehicles."

Phil added, "And those tripods, as you call them, can only work on smooth roads. Their wheels wouldn't make it over rough terrain."

"So," Andie said, a new thought entering her mind, "If the aliens really want to get all of the people, they will need to have something that moves over all kinds of land, or even water."

"We haven't seen any other devices or creatures, yet," said Phil. "But that's not to say they aren't out there."

Andie experienced a cold shiver of fear and wrapped her arms around herself.

"I'm sorry," Phil said. "I didn't mean to scare you. I was just teasing out the possibilities." He looked concerned, and Andie appreciated that, giving him a weak smile.

"No, no," she said. "It's okay. It's just that the horrors keep on coming."

Joe jumped up, and said, "Who wants to see a dead bear in the river?"

Andie laughed loudly. "Good way to change the subject, Joe."

Pat stood up, and said, "I'm game. Phil?"

Phil stayed seated and said, "No, I'm good. I'll stay here and keep Andie company."

"Listen, why don't I make a hearty meal before you head off to climb mountains?" Andie offered.

"Now that sounds great," Joe grinned at Andie. "We missed breakfast, and I, for one, am famished."

"We can always eat," Phil commented.

"But where do you put it?" Andie said. "You guys are so slim."

"Good genes," Pat imparted as he exited the cabin, with Joe and Satchmo following behind.

Andie stood up, and then walked over to the pile of canned foods. "Let's see." She held up a can of peaches. "Here's the fruit." Then she rooted around in the pile until she found a much larger can. "And here's the Dinty Moore beef stew."

"Awesome," Phil said. Andie opened the cans with a manual opener, one of several that Joe had acquired during his last trip into town. She poured the stew into a large pan to be placed over the fireplace. She deftly lit some kindling, and then worked to make a larger concentrated fire. After a few minutes, with one log beginning to catch the heat and spread, she hung the pan from the overhead rod above the fire.

"Okay," she sighed in satisfaction, "That shouldn't take too long."

"I'm impressed, "Phil said. "How long did you say you've been here?"

Andie pursed her lips, "Hmm. Maybe a week and a half? It feels longer but I haven't kept track of the days."

"So, you folks are going to weather the invasion out here by the stream?" Phil asked.

"I guess that's the plan. I thought maybe we would go to higher ground, too, especially after seeing all the spaceships, but no, we're staying here." She stared off into the distance.

"Something is telling me that you don't agree with that plan," Phil said. He cocked his head sideways, asking her for the information she wasn't stating.

"The problem is…" she began, but then faltered. "The problem is that we can't climb mountainsides with Satchmo. You saw what a chunk he is, and he's getting old. And he got hurt badly recently."

"Have you and Joe had him for long?" Phil asked.

"Oh!" Andie said. "No, he's not my dog. He belongs to Joe."

"And do you belong to Joe?"

"No! Well, yes, but no," Andie answered.

Phil just laughed. "That was an interesting answer that tells me absolutely nothing."

Andie smiled, a pink blush covering her cheeks and neck. She thought about the intimacy that she and Joe had shared, but she knew not to divulge that information. "Joe and I met at our apartment complex in Columbia, Maryland, on the first day the discs appeared. We decided to join forces to try and escape to the Allegheny Mountains. We've had some really horrible experiences, but we've stuck together. We kind of made a pact, friends until the end, whatever that end may be. We've helped each other. A lot. But we aren't a couple. Things are way too complicated right now. We just appreciate each other for who we are and how we can push through the tough stuff."

"Sort of the way my brother and I rely on each other. We have each other's backs, now and forever," Phil said.

"Yes, just like that," Andie smiled at Phil. "You know, it is so nice to speak to other people. I had forgotten how I need a sounding board sometimes."

"Don't we all?" Phil said. Andie turned to stir the stew and dish out the peaches into separate small bowls.

"Andie, what's up with your leg? I see it's wrapped up."

"You know that bear that your brother and Joe are checking out? He was the cause of an injury I had to my leg."

"Are you kidding me?" Phil looked at Andie in surprise.

"No, she's not kidding," Joe's voice interjected as he came through the door. "But the end of the story is that the bear is dead, and…"

"Andie is very much alive," Phil nodded in private assessment of the woman's strong abilities.

"Uh, right," Joe agreed with a searching expression. He felt something pass between Andie and Phil, and he wasn't sure he liked it.

"Time for brunch!" Andie called out. They all filled their bowls and then their bellies with the warm stew, enjoying the limited moments of conviviality and friendship.

# *CHAPTER 27*

As Satchmo licked up the remnants of the stew sticking to the sides in the pot, everyone filtered outside. Pat showed Joe and Andie his map of the park and the general route of where he and his brother were headed. The plateau they had decided on was only a few miles away, and they would use trail markers that the park had painted on selected trees. As the brothers gathered their backpacks and gear, they thanked Andie and Joe for their hospitality. Or as Pat said, "After this is all over, we can write a book and call it "Making Friends in the Time of Alien Invasions." They all laughed, and even Satchmo joined in with his wiggle dancing. Phil managed to pull Andie aside and whispered, "If you change your mind, you can meet up with us, okay?" His blue eyes radiated honesty, and Andie felt his concern. "You know the way now," he added. Andie just nodded and briefly reached out to clutch his shoulder. "Thanks," she said.

With the brothers hiking back into the woods, they were soon out of sight. Andie returned inside the cabin to clean up the dishes from their meal. Joe took the solar radio outside to attempt to find an audible station. Since the last time Andie had listened to the broadcast about the impending invasion, they hadn't been able to get any signal.

As Andie placed the last of the bowls on the shelf, Joe startled her as he said, "Hey."

"Hey, yourself. Any luck?" Andie asked.

"No. I'm pretty sure we've heard the last of the transmissions."

"That's pretty sad," Andie shook her head and stared at the floor.

"Andie, I want to tell you something. I need to tell you that if you want to go up the mountains, then you should. I don't want to hold you back, if that's what you really want to do. Satch and I will have to stay here, of course. I just don't think it's safe for him. But I feel like he and I will be fine here."

"Joe, I'm not leaving you. Or Satch. It wouldn't be right. We started this trip together, and we'll finish it together. I'm not someone who runs away from her promises or responsibilities." Andie took a deep breath. "We don't know what the future holds, but somehow we've managed to survive when many others didn't. Just forget about what I wanted before, and let's concentrate on getting through another day. Deal?" She extended her hand towards him.

"Deal," he answered and shook her hand.

They worked side by side to reorganize their stores of food and other supplies. Joe put together what he called 'go packs.' These were two backpacks filled with small food cans, medical supplies, a set of clothing for each and a sleeping bag tied to the handles. Joe felt that they needed to be ready for any attack on any front. Andie slid into the straps of the backpack and groaned at the weight of all the items inside.

"Yikes. I might make it ten feet with this." She was letting the backpack slip to the floor, when Joe grabbed her arm and said, "Listen!"

Together they heard an unusual sound, coming from above and not too far away. "I think it's a small spaceship," Joe whispered. "Get on the floor, and don't move." They both slid down and laid side by side. "*Tsk, tsk, tsk, tsk, tsk.*" The sound grew louder as the spaceship slowly moved over their cabin and the near woods. Within minutes, the sound faded into the distance.

"Let's stay here," Joe said. They remained on the floor, listening for any unusual sounds or movements. Andie turned on her side and met Joe's eyes. "I think the cabin passed the alien flyby test," she said. Joe nodded his head. "Maybe," he said.

And then they heard it again, coming from the direction it had gone, travelling back towards them. Andie closed her eyes and prayed. This time the spaceship seemed to have moved closer to the river and not over their cabin. It was soon gone from hearing range.

Andie stared at the ceiling, counting spider webs. The spaceship returned, even further away, on the other side of the stream and over that side of the woods.

"It's following a grid," Joe observed. "It's covering a large area from east to west, and every time it is more to the north. It seems like every 15 minutes or so it's in our parallel."

"But why?" Andie asked.

"Oh, Andie, do you really need to ask?" Joe's voice sounded tired and worn. "They're looking for us. And anyone else like us who is hiding in the park."

"But they didn't find us! We disguised the cabin enough so that they didn't know it's a people place."

They heard a monstrous noise, a sound that went from lower to high pitched in seconds, and then an explosion that rocked the earth their cabin was built upon. They didn't dare look outside, so they weren't certain, but in their hearts they both knew the source of the sound. The spaceship had blown up the rest stop only a few miles away.

"No more Big Meadows Lodge," Joe whispered.

Andie chewed on the inside of her mouth. She wondered if people had stopped there in the last few days, thinking it was a good and safe place to ride out the invasion.

"Skyline Hotel will be next," Joe added.

Andie stood up and walked over to Satchmo, who was cowering and shaking in the corner. "Come here, puppy. It's okay." She knelt and gathered him towards her lap, "Come and let me love you." She stroked his head and neck, crooning into his ears. "You're my favorite, you know that, right?"

"Hey, what does that make me?" Joe teased.

"Chopped liver," Andie said while hugging Satchmo. Then she buried her face into his fur.

Joe stood, staring at the covered window. "I sure hope Pat and Phil got away safely,"

"Mmhmm."

As Joe predicted, the next explosion was from the north, and the Skyland Hotel was presumed gone. The rest of the day and evening was uneventful, while they remained in their camouflaged cabin. Andie let her thoughts go in directions that left her shaking. She knew she shouldn't let her imagination stray while the reality of the aliens was horrible enough. But her only positive thought was that it was another day of living, such as it was.

# *CHAPTER 28*

The next morning was sunny and bright, and Andie wondered how much longer the fair weather would continue. Spring usually brought frequent rainstorms, but the skies had been clear since before she had left home. While Joe and Satchmo went for a walk, exploring the surrounding areas for wild berries, Andie grabbed the fishing pole and headed down to the stream. She noted that the water was still clear although a bit lower on the banks than the last time she had been there. She didn't let herself think about the bears or any other wild animals as she dug up worms and baited her hook. As she made her first cast into the water, she heard voices coming from behind her and up the drive. She watched as two older men negotiated the branches and brush that Joe had scattered across the driving path. She reeled in her line and placed her rod down on the ground, wiping her hands on her pants to clean off any soil remaining from her digging. She walked towards the men, feeling nervous and excited.

"Hey," she called. As the men approached, she recognized them and started laughing, "What brings you two down here?" It was Clifford and Lewis, the men from the coffee shop who had discussed camping in the woods with her.

"Hello, young lady," Clifford said. "We thought we'd pay you a visit and see how you're doing."

"How did you know where to find us?" she asked.

"Why, June at Ed's restaurant told us. We were having our morning coffee and eggs like usual, and we got to talking about how we could live in the woods, if we had to."

"But I thought you had already decided to do that with tents and all."

Lewis shook his head and clucked his tongue. "Coming up with a plan, and actually doing it are two different things entirely, especially when you have to take into account our women folk."

"Your woman, Lewis. Don't get Donna involved in this. She was open to the idea of moving into the woods until Susie said she wouldn't go," Clifford said.

"If only those women weren't so stubborn," Lewis said.

"If only one of them didn't have to do whatever the other did," Clifford grumbled. He turned to Andie. "They've been friends for decades, and they won't be separated. We're going to have to take our chances living in town."

"But how did you escape that tripod thing that patrols the road?" Andie asked.

"What tripod thing?" Clifford said.

"Oh, boy," Andie took a deep breath and gestured toward the cabin. "Come on in for a drink. Coffee? Water? And how did you get here?"

Lewis said, "We'll take some water, and we drove my truck here. We left it at the top of the drive."

"Yeah, we didn't want to chance it getting stuck in that overgrowth," said Clifford.

The men sat in the chairs Andie offered them, and she poured water from a gallon jug Joe had found for them. "My partner, Joe, is out and about with his dog. It will give Satchmo a nice workout, and maybe they'll find something edible for us."

Lewis drained his glass of water and placed it on the table. "I'm not sure it's the right time of year for much of anything, but I guess it's worth a try."

Andie perched on the edge of the mattress. "Listen, aren't you guys worried about the aliens? Not only is there the tripod that travels the highway and shoots lasers at cars, but there's also a spaceship that flew over here a few days ago. We think it fired on the lodges up on Shenandoah Drive."

"Oh, sure. We passed Big Meadows today, and it's just rubble. Nothing left, really," Lewis said.

"It's a darned shame," added Clifford.

"So what are you going to do?" asked Andie.

"Do? We're not doing anything, just as I said. We're staying in our homes and hoping for the best. But we aren't stupid, and Lewis and I both know our time is limited. We've lived good, long lives, and if it is our time to go, then so be it."

Andie felt tears prick at her eyes, and she sat quietly. She understood what the men were saying, that this brutal change that had come to everyone was hard and nearly impossible to face, but it made her frustrated that they weren't going to try to fight to save themselves.

"Well, missy," Clifford said as he put his glass down, "I guess we'll be on our way. It looks like you have enough food and supplies to last a good while. I wish luck to you and your young man." He crossed the room to shake Andie's hand.

"Thanks for stopping by. Do you need anything? We can share some of our food."

"No, no. We're doing just fine," Clifford said as he and Lewis stood in the doorway.

"Take care of yourself. Watch out for that tripod, okay?" Andie said.

"See you, Miss. Maybe we'll catch up again, after the big invasion," Lewis said.

"That…would be nice." Andie knew in her heart of hearts that this would probably be the last time she saw the older gentlemen. She wanted to stay in the cabin and weep, but instead she walked back to the stream to continue fishing. It was impossible to guess how long the weather would hold, and Andie was going to 'make hay while the sun shines.'

# CHAPTER 29

Joe and Andie were at the stream, bathing themselves and Satchmo in the heat of midday. The water was cold still but it didn't deter them from jumping in. Satchmo joined them but had to be held while soap was applied to his fur. He scrabbled on the rocks whenever his feet could find purchase. As soon as he was rinsed and released, he swam to the dirt bank and then shook the water droplets off his back, making a small rainbow in the sunshine. Andie and Joe shared the bar of soap and washed themselves while still wearing their undergarments. Modesty was still an issue with Andie, though Joe would have gladly shucked his jockeys into the bushes. Joe teased Andie by sending a splash, and she playfully returned the gesture. They were both laughing with water dripping into their eyes when Satchmo began to bark. Andie had learned Satch's different barks, and this one was his signal of impending danger.

Andie and Joe both waded over to the side of the stream bank where the foliage was thick. They hid behind the reeds and bushes and peered through the openings in the greenery. Nothing could have prepared them for the grotesque sight before them. Two beings, approximately five feet tall, cavorted in the open meadow. They were stick-thin with arms and legs in the right places, but they were clearly not humans. Each creature had no covering and resembled a praying mantis in color and shape, except without the wings. Their heads were ovoid, and their eyes were red, a bright glaring crimson. Andie, still partially in the stream, recognized the eyes as the same as the ones she had seen in Columbia with Officer Frank. She began to shake from the chilly water and the fear engendered by those eyes. Joe moved towards her and pulled her into his arms.

The alien creatures began clacking their claw-like hands back and forth to each other. Satchmo seemed enchanted by his new friends and weaved around and through their stick legs. One alien leaned down and stroked Satchmo's back with his claw. Satchmo dropped to the ground and turned on to his back, inviting a belly rub. The aliens walked away, leaving Satch looking around and wondering why he was being ignored.

Andie took deep shuddering breaths. She knew that as tolerant as the aliens were with Satchmo, humans would not receive the same benevolent attention.

The aliens pushed open the cabin door and went inside.

"Oh, god, no," Andie whispered. "They're going to know that humans live there. The food, the bed, the chairs, everything spells human."

"Shh," Joe said. He had begun shaking from the cold water as well. "Let's just wait and see."

Satchmo appeared in an opening in the bushes right next to Andie and Joe, his tail wagging.

"Shoo," Joe said. "Go back." He waved his arms in the direction of the cabin. Satchmo, thinking Joe was playing a game, started barking.

The aliens appeared in the doorway of the cabin, peering around the area with their pulsing eyes. They noted Satchmo, then walked into the field in front of the cabin, clicking their claws.

"I can't do this much longer," Andie said. "I'm freezing."

Fortunately, within a few minutes, the aliens left the immediate area, walking away through the tall grasses. Andie crawled out on to the stream bank and rubbed her hands up and down her arms and legs to regain some feeling in her frozen limbs. Joe followed suit, but neither of them moved away from the protection of the plants for some time.

"I think they're gone," Andie said.

"Yeah, but now that they know we live here, they'll be back."

"Maybe not. They didn't seem curious enough to look for us, and we were just yards away."

"That's true. Maybe they're just opportunistic killers. They only go for the easy prey," Joe said. Andie shook her head and gave Joe a searching look.

"Really? Do you honestly believe that?"

"No. But it beats thinking that we're going to be hunted down and killed in cold blood while we sleep tonight."

Andie stood up and squeezed water from her hair. "Nice, Joe, real nice."

"Damn, but they were ugly," Joe said.

"And how do they do anything with those hands?" Andie wondered.

"They have the ability to traverse space, and yet they look like something out of a Sunday morning cartoon."

"In a way, that makes them scarier. We can't underestimate them just because they look weird."

"It's possible that those two beings are different from others of their species."

"Maybe." Andie couldn't make sense of what she'd seen. "Wasn't it strange how they seemed to like Satchmo?"

"When we were home, we saw how they allowed animals to live while they went after humans. They ignored squirrels and birds."

"That one alien actually touched Satch. It was…revolting." Andie walked towards the cabin, scanning the surrounding areas. "And I'm creeped out that they were in our cabin."

"We're going to have to figure out what to do next. Our safety has been compromised."

"You mean our 'illusion' of safety," Andie said.

"Yeah, that," Joe agreed.

# *CHAPTER 30*

As Andie and Joe finished up their supper of canned fruit and boxed graham crackers, the earth rumbled under their feet. It came with a deep percussive sound and caused Joe and Andie to grab onto anything heavy and stable-in this case the fireplace for Joe and the bed for Andie. Satch's eyes were wide and rounded. He felt the vibrations more than anyone, and it didn't make him happy.

"What the hell is that?" Andie asked.

Joe shook his head, as perplexed as Andie. "Let me go see."

"I'll blow out the candles. We need to be dark… in case." She didn't have to explain the why or the what. Anything was possible at this point. With the flying discs, the tripod robots, the incinerating spaceships, and the stick-like aliens, there were a lot of reasons to exercise caution. Andie blew out the candles scattered around the room and squeezed the wicks to stop any smoke. "Okay," she said.

Joe unlocked the door and opened it a few inches to peer around and out into the glen. The ground was still shaking, sometimes hard, sometimes less, providing a chance to walk outdoors. Joe looked to the north west, where a barrage of lights and sounds penetrated the night sky. He could see a mothership high in the sky, perhaps as high as the stratosphere, and although it was far away, there was no mistaking its outline or the laser-like rays shooting from its underside. Andie stood right behind Joe, gawking at the spaceship.

"Shit! Andie, you've got to see this," Joe called. He jumped when Andie said, "I'm right behind you."

Andie closed the cabin door to keep Satchmo inside and kept her gaze on the mother ships, or as they had previously dubbed them, the planet killers.

"What are they doing? I mean, what are they destroying? What's their target?" Andie couldn't stop the flow of questions that were falling from her lips. "What cities are in that direction, Joe? It's Washington, D.C., right? What else is there?"

"All of the Northern Virginia towns and cities. The ship could be targeting any of them. Or all of them. Even Baltimore."

Andie gasped, "Baltimore? That's close to Columbia!"

"So is D.C., for that matter."

"We need to get higher so that we can see what's happening. We could climb some of those hills, maybe. The ones the guys went to," Andie said. She shook with each booming noise and the explosions that came from the attacks.

"Yeees. I guess we could," Joe said.

"Come on, Joe! We need information. It's the only thing that's going to help us," Andie pleaded.

"Okay. Let me get a flashlight and my gun."

Andie nodded. "I think I'll change into dark pants to keep better camouflaged."

They both returned to the cabin to grab their gear and change clothes. Joe spent a minute with Satchmo, sitting at his side and petting him. "We'll be back soon, boy. You just rest and take a snooze."

Once out of the cabin again, with the door latched, and walking through the tall grass and weeds, Joe held the flashlight down low to the ground so that the range of the illumination was limited. It was rough going through the fallen tree limbs and occasional rocks, but they reached the foot of the first hill after about fifteen minutes.

"If you thought that was tough, wait until we climb this baby." Joe indicated the uneven terrain and the slippery rock faces of the hill.

"Let's just do it. I can't think about how steep it is. I just have to do it." Andie looked at Joe, resolute in her decision to climb. Joe gave her an understanding smile.

"You go first," Joe directed. "That way if you slip or fall, I can try to catch you."

"Deal," Andie replied. She knew she was vulnerable with her weakened leg. She began her ascent, placing one foot in front of the other. She scanned for easy footholds, or even handholds, as she went. One time, she even got to her knees and crawled in the dirt until she reached an area that could allow her to be upright. The shaking of the earth never stopped, and it made their climb even harder than it should have been.

"Hey!" Andie called to Joe. "I think that tree has markings. Phil said they would put some paint on the tree trunks to show the path they took to the top of the mountain."

"We won't be climbing as high as they have, but it will probably help us find the best path through the trees," Joe said.

Andie finally made her way to a level that had a wide rock ledge, with enough space for both of them to sit and gain a better view of the mothership.

"Here," she said. "Is this good enough for us?" She let Joe pass her and slide sideways on to the ledge.

He sighed. "Oh, yeah. Come on over."

She squeezed down beside him and worked to catch her breath. It hadn't been a hard climb, but it had been upwards all the way.

They both turned to view the spaceship and the rays of destruction that emanated from it. They watched the mother ship moving and sending blasts of pinkish purple energy towards targeted areas. They couldn't see the cities from their perch, but they could tell from the pulsing rays, the rumbling earth, and the crashing they heard even at this distance, that civilization was under attack. They had known that the aliens meant business; they had experienced so much horror of their own in the last few weeks. But seeing the methodical manner which the ship was extinguishing city after city was beyond belief and understanding.

"The people! What about all those people?" Andie trembled, and Joe snaked his arm around her shoulders.

"We can't survive this," she said. "They are killing every single person on Earth. I'm sure the other mother ships are doing the same on other continents."

Joe nodded in agreement. "Yes. I'm sure they are. In a few weeks, or even days, they will have managed to wipe out all signs of our existence. But I'm telling you again, Andie. They can't get us all. There is no way that they can ferret out each and every human being. Or even every house or cabin. Look at us. We're still here, and as far as I'm concerned, we will still be here at the end."

"Oh?" Andie didn't have a trace of belief left in her. "That mothership is destroying buildings that house hundreds of people, maybe thousands. The aliens are even killing pets, and those are animals which they previously seemed to ignore. What about the zoos in the big cities? Those animals will be killed alongside their keepers. That is, if any people stayed, with the other alien contraptions buzzing around."

"I know. The cities are just target practice right now. But I can't help but believe that there are lots of others like us, maybe even here in this valley that are doing a good job hiding. And maybe, someday, we'll be able to meet up and start new," Joe said.

"If the aliens leave, maybe so. But what if they're here to stay? Maybe they want the Earth all to themselves. Then our chances of survival are nil," Andie slapped her hands together in a loud burst. She turned her back on the distant devastation.

"We can only wait and see." Joe said. He pulled Andie closer to him, and she rested her head on his shoulder.

"Maybe you and I will be the founders of a new order on this planet. Maybe we'll have children, and they will find others to marry and have families."

Tears began to trail down Andie's cheeks. "Oh, Joe. Even during an apocalypse, you are a romantic."

Joe laughed. "What better time? Hey, if we manage to get through this, we deserve a happy ending."

Andie swiped at her tears with the back of her hand, "Yes, I guess we do."

The grumbling and movement of the ground seemed to have lessened as the mother ship moved further north.

"We better get back," Andie commented. "Satch will be going crazy."

"I think that if we write our memoirs, it should be called Andie, Joe and Satch Save the World," Joe said.

"Oh my God," Andie said. "And you want to be the father of my children? I'm going to have to think about this."

Joe started down the side of the hill. Andie took a deep breath and followed behind. She twisted her ankle slightly on a loose rock and muttered. "Frickin' rock."

"Hey, I heard that!" he whispered.

"You're going to hear a whole lot more than that, if this keeps up."

Joe smiled to himself. "Of that, I have no doubt."

# CHAPTER 31

By the following morning, the ground vibrations had lessoned as the giant spaceships moved further and further away from the Shenandoah Valley. There were no overhead spacecraft searching for homes and manmade buildings; they heard no sounds coming from the main drive up the hill. In all, the day harkened back to when they first arrived, with the only change appearing in the gathering clouds above. The area was due for rain. It had been a dry spell for this time of year. Joe went outside to reconnoiter the surrounding area and the skies for signs of extraterrestrials, but it appeared to be a day that could give them time to regroup, and maybe relax. Andie's face was buried deep in another Ray Bradbury book, *The Martian Chronicles*. She was highly aware of the irony that she was reading science fiction while living through an alien apocalypse. Satchmo was pacing the interior of the cabin, nosing in the food supplies for loose food treats. Andie was just about to call Satch to her side when the cabin door opened and Joe stood holding a bouquet of wildflowers.

"For you, dear girl," and he held them towards Andie with a flourish. Andie laughed and stood to gather the flowers into her arms. "You shouldn't have! But I'm glad you did. Let me get a jar to put them in." As she turned to the cabinets, Satchmo wove through various boxes and chair legs and ran straight through the open doorway.

"Satch!" Joe yelled. "Get back here, boy!" But Satchmo must have sighted a rabbit or squirrel because he was off into the brush in seconds. Andie had turned when Joe had called out to the dog and decided to give chase. She handed the flowers to Joe and ran across the open green space to the field to the right of the cabin. "Satch!" she called. "Come back, boy!" She had a glimpse of his short wiggly legs just a few yards ahead. She stopped. The dog would return on his own. He always did, eventually. So, she stood for a second to catch her breath. That's when she realized that there were no other sounds around her. All the birds and buzzing insects were quiet. Perhaps it was because of the storm that had been gathering in the clouds. Andie looked back at the cabin and saw that Joe was still in the doorway holding his flowers, doing a visual search for Satchmo. That was when Andie heard it. The clunking sound of a heavy moving thing, the pound of metallic feet on the dirt, the whirring of parts and pieces of an unknown machine. She fell to her knees, and then her stomach, among the weeds and low plants. She lifted her head and saw the metal monster at the same time as Joe did. It pushed through the woods and stood motionless, its aperture wide and pointed at Joe. Joe turned his head in Andie's direction and said, "Andie." The aperture instantly turned from black to red, and a fiery ray blasted out at Joe. Andie watched as Joe was silhouetted in flames, and then incinerated to ashes. His burnt remains and those of the flowers he held were mixed together for eternity.

Andie laid her head in the dirt, and tried to keep breathing, even when the rain began to fall from above and made the ground wet and muddy. The metal monster left the area. Its heat ray had gone through Joe and blasted the back of the cabin, causing the walls to fall inwards, the roof to come crumbling down.

Andie began to claw at the ground, deeper and deeper, her fingernails filled with the rich earth. She began to cry tears of unrelenting grief, her body shaking in shock. "Joe," she called. "Joe."

She wanted him and needed him to protect her and care for her. There couldn't be a world without Joe. She couldn't continue in this world of violence and death alone.

Andie looked down at her legs when she felt something huddle against her. It was Satch. She pulled him up to her side and continued lying on the ground in the spring rain. "Satch," she murmured. "He's gone, buddy. Joe's gone." And they laid together for a long while, giving comfort to each other until both her tears and the rain stopped.

Finally, Andie drew herself up to her knees and looked around the area. She neither saw nor heard anything unusual so she stood, feeling weak and unsteady on her stiff legs. She walked towards the cabin, with Satchmo at her heels. When she reached the place where the doorway had been, she looked down and saw Joe's ashes under the wood of the door, protected from the rain. "Good," she nodded. Satchmo sniffed the ground once, but fortunately didn't seem to recognize the remains as those of his loving master.

Andie began to dig around the broken and splintered boards that had been the foundation of her temporary home. She found a random plastic bag and slowly pushed Joe's ashes inside it with the side of her book. She sealed the bag and stood gazing at the wreckage. There was a lot that was still salvageable; there were tins of food scattered all over the area. She could see some bowls and spoons in the mess. The bed was destroyed, but there was a pillow. She supposed the alien creature didn't really have the cabin as its main target. She was fortunate for that. And now, she knew what she had to do.

Andie gathered whatever was still useable and made a pile beside the cabin. Then she hacked her way into the woods where her Rav 4 was buried in brush and debris. She pulled away the dead branches on the rear passenger's side and yanked hard at the door. It opened, and Andie felt such incredible relief that she had to fight the urge to crawl in and collapse on the back seat. Instead, she carried the food tins, utensils, bowls, pillow, filled backpacks, and other survival goods that she would need. She filled the front passenger's seat and footwell, as well as the large area that the car provided when the back passengers' seats were pushed down.

She was exhausted and numb by the late afternoon, and so she gathered Satchmo up and placed him beside her in the car in a nest of soft materials that had dried in the sun over the past several hours. She fed Satch from his big bag of dried food, and she drank a Coke that had survived the devastation. She nibbled on a few Oreo cookies, thinking back to the time when she and Joe had hidden in her apartment in Columbia, really only a few weeks ago, when the alien nightmare was just beginning. Then she sank down onto her sleeping bag, gathered Satch into her arms and fell into a dreamless sleep.

# *CHAPTER 32*

Andie was unsure of the passing of time. She saw daylight and twilight and the dead of night, but she couldn't make sense of how long she spent sequestered in the Rav 4. She got out of the car to empty her bladder, or to allow Satch time to run around outdoors, tethered to a rope that only allowed him about eight feet of freedom. She ate whatever was in her grasp, usually crackers or chips, anything to keep her hunger at bay. Andie knew that she was suffering, and she was helpless to stop it. Eventually, she too got out of the car and walked around the field, extending her wandering to the stream and the fresh water. When she finally bathed in the cold, refreshing stream on a warm morning that seemed safe and comfortable, she felt renewed. The healing process had begun.

She once again explored the wreckage of the cabin and found a few more salvageable pieces to pack into the car. When she found the small garden shovel, she knew that it was time to bury Joe and honor him with a simple ceremony. She dug a deep hole in a place by the field where she had been hiding when he had been killed. It was only a few feet away from Miss Bey's grave, which she and Joe had dug the first week they had been at the cabin. With Satchmo trotting around the loose pile of dirt and chasing a monarch butterfly into the tall weeds, she lowered the bag of Joe's remains into the hole. She blew a kiss, and said, "I will never forget you, Joe. You were a strong and loyal friend, a sweet man and a true fighter. I'll tell people about you so that your story will carry on. You were a true hero." With tears running down her cheeks, she shoveled the loose dirt into the grave. Then she pushed the shovel into the dirt beside the disturbed earth, deep down so that only the handle remained above the ground. It would be a marker for Joe's grave, until she could find a more fitting tribute. In a way, it seemed appropriate that it was a shovel for it symbolized how hard Joe had worked to keep them safe from the aliens.

She couldn't stop herself from thinking about the precious times she had spent with Joe. The way he had saved her in the garbage area of her apartment complex when the first disc had come upon them. How he had shot at the men at

Skyland and saved Satchmo. When he had taken care of her after her incident with the bear. And when he stood in the doorway of the cabin, holding the wildflowers he had picked for her. Now she would never know if they could have had a future together. He had wanted to have children, and Andie knew that he would have made an incredible father. Would she and Joe have bonded together over time? She hadn't known how she felt about Joe when they had been together, and she would never know now.

Andie rubbed her hands to wipe off the dirt and turned to view her surroundings. It was so serene that it was hard to believe that such horror and devastation had occurred in this little corner of the world. And yet it had. Andie knew she must remain vigilant to keep herself and Satch hidden.

So many types of aliens, the discs, the highway rollers, the small spaceships, the metal walkers, not to mention the gigantic mother ships, all geared to destroy human civilization. Humans were clearly the target, but why? Andie knew that any of the greatest minds on Earth that managed to survive were working on that very question. There were several possibilities that even Andie could surmise. The aliens wanted to take over Earth and live there themselves. Or there were resources on Earth that the aliens wanted for themselves. But Andie had a hunch that the reasons for the alien invasion were more complicated than that. Maybe the aliens were descendants of the creatures that originally populated the Earth. Perhaps these descendants were displeased with the way humans had evolved and how we treated one another. All of this seemed possible to Andie, as much as any other rationale for the total eradication of the human race.

Andie realized that she couldn't stay at the cabin area. Eventually she would run out of provisions. The seasons would pass, and she needed shelter. She also needed human interaction. She was living in a state of sadness and fear. She could try to drive the Rav 4 out of the woods and up the hill to the road, but the aliens would surely find her there. She knew the towns surrounding the park were probably destroyed, and the people as well. Her recourse was to find the twins, Pat and Phil, up on the mountainside. Phil had invited her to join their camp, hadn't he? But would the men still be there?

The thought of being with others gave Andie a glimmer of hope that thawed her heart. She knew what she had to do next. She gazed at Satchmo, wondering how to solve the problem of getting him up the steep ridges of the mountain. Satchmo was too heavy to carry, especially with her unpredictable leg. Satch wouldn't put up with some type of sling anyway. But Satch must be saved, of that she had no doubt. Satch had protected her and Joe, and he deserved to be given a chance to live as well. He had been Joe's companion, and that meant he was Joe's legacy.

She would attempt the climb alone. She would be able to move faster and more carefully if she went by herself, without Satch. Satch would be left at the cabin area with enough food and water to survive for a day, no more than that. A rope could be tied to the undercarriage of the car, and then the other end could be tied to Satchmo's leash. The Rav was high off the ground so that Satch could rest and find shelter under it if he was threatened by an animal or alien. Andie filled a can with water from the stream and dug a hole to provide support around the can so that Satch would be unable to spill its precious contents. She filled a large bowl with dried dog food, knowing he would eat it all as soon as she left. But that food would last him a day without any hunger to bother him.

Andie grabbed one of the survival backpacks that she and Joe had packed before his death, and flung it around her shoulders and slipped her arms through the straps. It was heavy, but it had everything she needed to survive. Or so she hoped. She also put on a waist pack and slipped in Joe's gun, which she had found among the rubble of the cabin.

Andie gave Satchmo a fierce hug and told him how much she loved him. "I'll be back, Satch. Don't worry. Take some long naps in the cool woods or under the car." Then she kissed his furry ears and walked away without a backward glance. She was sure that Satchmo was already digging into his early dinner.

# *CHAPTER 33*

Andie walked through fields of green grasses, glancing in all directions to ascertain her safety from the aliens and random strangers. At the foothill of the mountain, she glanced upwards and realized that the mountain path was much clearer than she remembered from when she and Joe had gone to watch the alien firestorms. She followed the bare earth of the footpath, sidestepping loose stones and tree roots as she climbed. In very short order, she found the ledge where she and Joe had talked about their future and had spent time sharing thoughts. She sat for a while, sipping from a bottle of water and surveying the land from her higher perspective. She watched an eagle soar in the slight breeze and wondered if it had a nest of new eaglets higher above. And then, cognizant of the need to make contact with the twins before nightfall and her need to keep her time away from Satchmo brief, she resumed her climbing.

There were always trees marked with red, just as the men has said they would do, so that Andie never strayed far from the pathway for long. The trees were yards apart and not easily seen from one marked tree to the next. But she kept to her course, hoping upon hope that the men were still at the plateau, where they said they would be. The metal monsters that walked wouldn't make it up through the rough terrain, but the small spaceships could have scouted a visible camp from above. Andie wondered why she hadn't seen any sign of aliens in the last few days. She was thankful for that, but it made her nervous. She spotted a deer through the bushes at one point but startled it away as her boots made crackling sounds on the fallen tree branches. When the sun was high and the day had become hot, Andie stopped under a leafy tree to rest and eat some food packets. She felt like she had been walking for hours but she couldn't be certain. She was so tired that it felt good to lie down in the grass and just let herself be. But she couldn't allow herself to indulge in this pleasure for long, and soon picked up her backpack and continued on the trail. There were stretches of plain uphill rocks and compacted dirt, but there were also areas of green woods and flowering plants. She felt like Alice in Wonderland when she slipped through the lush green woods, bird calls above her and tall ferns around her. But her focus was on the trees with the red splatter marks. She would find the men.

Andie broke out of a wooded area and found herself on a wide flat stone at the crest of the mountain. She dropped her backpack down and raised her arms to catch the wind that danced across the plateau. She could see in a complete circle, with every inch of the park in view. As she twirled around, soaking in the sunshine and feeling lighter than she had in weeks, or even months, she heard a voice from behind her.

"Well, hey! Look who's here!" Andie whipped around to see Phil standing under a copse of trees, grinning wide and very much alive.

"Phil!" she yelled, and then ran the short distance down the hill and into his arms. "It is Phil, isn't it? Not Pat?"

"You got it in one. Wait a minute, girl. What's going on?" Phil laughed at her impetuous actions, but then sobered when he saw that Andie had tears in her eyes. "Hey…" he said.

"They came," Andie croaked, her voice tight with emotion. "The bastard aliens came and they got Joe. A metal monster pulverized him into ashes.

It destroyed the cabin." She was shaking as she related the nightmarish events.

"Oh my God," Phil whispered. "I am so sorry."

"I know; I know," Andie said. "But I hid in the grass, and they didn't get me. And Satchmo! Satchmo is alive! I left him down at the cabin with food and water, but I have to go back tomorrow."

"Come with me," Phil loosened his grasp on Andie and beckoned her further down into the woods. Andie picked up her backpack, then followed Phil a short way into an area thick with overgrown foliage. "Pat!" Phil called. Phil's twin popped out of a tent that had a camouflage tarp to make it almost invisible to the naked eye.

"Look what the wind blew in," Phil indicated Andie to Pat.

Pat made his way over to Andie and gave her a side hug. "How's it going?"

Andie hugged him in return, then stepped away and looked at the ground. "It's pretty awful."

Phil offered the information. "Pat, Joe's gone. The… aliens got him."

Pat's eyes widened. "They came to your camp?"

Andie looked up. "Yes, and now I'm here to ask for help and figure out what to do next."

"Let's get inside the tent. It's comfortable," said Phil.

Once inside the large tent, which had air holes at the top allowing the breezes to flow through, the threesome shared their experiences of the last week.

Phil commiserated with Andie's pain, saying, "I can't believe that you had to witness Joe's death. I know you two were close."

Andie nodded. "We were, but in a way that evolved from our survival. It's like we felt that we were the last two people on Earth who would survive. We took comfort in each other. And we also had the physical attraction, too, but that went nowhere. I have no idea what our relationship would have become if he hadn't died."

"It will probably take a while to figure out the whole thing, and hopefully you'll have the time to do it," Pat smiled and reached to touch Andie's hand.

"Hopefully," Andie smiled. "Although that sounds kind of like a pessimistic view wrapped in good wishes."

"Sorry. I've been alone here with my brother too long, and I'm losing my social graces," Pat said.

"We've all become a bit wild, if you ask me." Phil just shook his head.

"We have to be, don't we?" Andie asked. "We've had to give up most of our conveniences and luxuries and now we're living in a state park with the animals and the bare minimum for shelter."

"You said the aliens destroyed your cabin?" Phil asked.

"Is that right?" Pat said.

Andie felt that Pat was being reserved, and so she just nodded.

"What about the dog? What was his name?" Pat questioned.

"Satchmo is alive. I left him tied up in the shade with food and water. If another bear doesn't come crashing through, he should be okay for a while. And I managed to salvage all of the food cans and goods that made it through the laser explosion. I don't know why the metal monster didn't vaporize the entire cabin, but I think it was just after living people, and the wreckage was a byproduct."

Andie sighed. "I've put all the stuff in the Rav 4 in the woods. If I can get out of here, the car is packed and ready to go. I've been sleeping in there, too."

"Well, our car is still in the tunnel not far from your cabin on Skyline Drive," noted Pat. "We actually went there to check on it a few days ago. We got some food and more clothing. And we found a more direct route to the car from here than we used the first time when we met you and Joe."

"What I want to know is-why is it so quiet? I haven't seen or heard a spaceship or alien in two days," Andie said.

"I know," said Phil. "We noticed that as well."

"Something must be in the works," said Pat. "Maybe they'll take over the Earth."

"And I think they're getting ready to leave," said Phil. "They've probably killed as many people as they had planned on, and now they're going to head on back to… wherever they came from."

"I hope you're right," Andie said. "Because the other scenario is too scary to even consider. Have you seen the creatures? They are so strange, all arms and legs and a spherical head on top. And those red eyes! The aliens scare the hell out of me. They almost seem humanoid, and yet not."

"That's why I think they aren't staying," said Phil. "Is the Earth hospitable to them?"

"You do have a good point," Pat said to his brother. "But these aliens are impossible to predict. The technology we've seen has been so different from anything we've seen before."

Andie nodded, and said, "So, what do we do next? We can't live here forever. Cold weather comes after summer, and this tent isn't much protection. My cabin could probably be rebuilt but it would need a lot of wood in the winter to keep the fireplace going."

"I think we're going to have to wait a little longer before we make any decisions," Pat said. "We have to have all the information we can before we leave. You understand, right, Andie?"

"Sure," said Andie. "You guys have any food I can sink my teeth into? I'm starving!"

# *CHAPTER 34*

The twins and Andie pulled together a meal of vacuum-packed beef sticks and cheese with canned green bean. All the food was cold because no one wanted to risk drawing attention with fire and smoke from a campfire, but it still tasted wonderful. The boys even had a chocolate bar to share with Andie. The chocolatey richness made her groan with pleasure. She soon felt full and satisfied by the meal that they had generously shared with her. They spent a few hours talking about their home towns and notable hole-in-the-wall restaurants, creating a respite from a harrowing day.

Their lives prior to the invasion now seemed the stuff of dreams. Could they have taken so much for granted? They marveled over electricity, fast food, instant communication, television-even soft beds and pillows! As their conversation wound down, each fell asleep among the fiberfill sleeping bags. It was a lovely night with a mild temperature and silence in the woods all around them.

In the small hours of the morning, Andie left the tent to relieve herself. Afterwards, she made her way to the plateau and looked up at the stars. She gasped when she saw a light show that exceeded the power of the galaxy around her. Several motherships were rising into the blackness of the outer reaches of the atmosphere. There were so many alien ships that they blotted out the regular constellations.

Andie screamed in excitement to the brothers, "Pat! Phil! Get out here! Now!"

She heard the men rustling in the tent but didn't dare move her eyes away from the spectacle above her. She began to see smaller spaceships, like the one that had flown overhead the cabin and destroyed the lodges on the Skyline Drive. These ships were streaming upwards in lines by the thousands and appearing to be absorbed into the motherships. Even the smaller craft that had first landed in towns and cities were making their way upwards.

"Holy shit!" Phil exclaimed. He stood beside Andie, his eyes flashing with exhilaration.

"Damn straight," Pat said. "Looks like you were right, Phil. They are definitely leaving."

Andie grabbed an arm of each man. "Do you really think so?"

"Look at all of those ships. My god, Earth never stood a chance," Phil said.

Andie felt tears slipping down her cheeks. "I wish Joe was here to see this. This is what we worked for-to make it through. But he didn't, and I don't know how I can be happy."

Phil put his arm around her shoulders. "It's okay to be happy and sad at the same time."

Andie looked up into Phil's eyes. With horror, she saw the pulsing of an alien's red eyes. She pulled away from Phil and screamed. "You! What the hell are you?" She looked at Pat, and his eyes also held the demonic red as he stood still with his head cocked strangely to one side. Within seconds, the weird eye color disappeared from both men, and their pupils went back to their previous blue.

"Are you aliens? Are you?" She pulled Joe's gun from her waist pouch and aimed it at the men. Her breathing was jagged, and she felt light-headed. She stepped backwards, trying to keep her arm straight and steady. "I'll kill you. I will."

Phil took a step forward, then thought better of it and moved back to his original position. "Andie, don't! It's not what you think."

"I think you're aliens. I saw your eyes, you monsters! Your eyes turned red and did that side-to-side thing that I've seen other aliens do."

"We're different. I swear." Pat stretched out an arm in supplication. "We're part human. We are sympathizers with the human race. We wouldn't hurt you or any human being."

Andie looked at Phil. "Is that true? Or are you going to blast me with those red eyes you're hiding?"

"We've had many opportunities to eradicate you but we haven't, have we? Even that first time we saw you and Joe down at the cabin, we could have ended you then."

"Why didn't you? Is this some kind of game for you?" Andie felt like screaming again but she fought an internal battle to stay calm. She would seek retribution for Joe's death if the twins made any wrong move. "Explain yourselves," she ordered.

Phil nodded. "You are right. We are aliens, descendent from a species that exists outside of your solar system. We are related to the aliens that are in the skies right now, but we are not them. Our original purpose has been to take note of human behavior since the beginning of the last century. There are dozens of 'Communicators' like us who have integrated into Earth's societies and gathered information that has been shared with our leaders. Our vessels have visited Earth briefly to take our information and carry it back to our home world. Of course, there has been the occasional human who has spotted the spacecraft, or saucers, as you call them."

"How do you have human form?" Andie asked.

"We have a way of entering a human body and becoming a part of it. If you viewed our naked backs, you would see the zipper scar that extends from our neck and down to the bottom of our spine," Pat said.

Andie shuddered then yelled, "You take living people and make them into aliens? That's barbaric!"

"That's where you're wrong. Once the melding takes place, we become equal parts human and alien. The human part continues to exist, and it reaps the benefits of its alien half like a longer life and immunities to various diseases."

"In theory," said Phil. "But actually our human part has taken over our alien part, and we have become as vulnerable as you to our current iterations. We have no interest in destroying the human race, and yet we understand our brothers' motives."

"Which are?" Andie asked. This is the question that had bothered her from the start of the alien infestation.

Phil closed his eyes for a few seconds. When he reopened them, they were filled with sorrow. "Shall we go through the list of horrors you've enacted on this world? Pollution of every form has caused global climate change. And the climate change is endangering every living thing. You've done nothing but suck out the earth's resources. The countdown clock on Earth's extinction is at zero. You did this to your own planet. The human race has methodically destroyed the Earth. Our brethren want to return the Earth to its natural state, which would only be possible if mankind were not there to consume and pollute."

"We have a vested interest in Earth because it is the planet that most resembles our home world. It has the correct elements that would ensure our survival if we needed to leave our own planet. We have a cautious understanding of space and are aware that any stray asteroid could threaten a world by knocking it even slightly off its path. Earth is the planet we've chosen to use in the event of a catastrophic event. We don't want it ruined."

"The methods our brothers used are more brutal than we ever would have expected. We never would have informed them of Earth's problems if we had known that humans would be destroyed. You see, we are humans, too, and we want to survive."

"You know," Andie said, "I always believed that extraterrestrial beings had been here before. I thought they were the ones who may have even brought humans to this planet. Now I see that these fellow aliens are acting like demonic caretakers, and they don't like what we've done with Earth."

"That is correct. Their actions show that they believe the Earth will recover now that the majority of humans are gone," Pat said.

"I don't know what to do," said Andie as she lowered her gun.

"Give us a chance to show you how we can help you. We survivors will all need to band together. It's the only thing that makes sense," said Phil.

Andie continued holding the gun at her side. "I don't trust you. How could I? You have alien DNA running through your veins. But I don't think I can make it on my own in this new world. I'm going to keep my eyes on you."

"We have a long road ahead of us," Pat commented. "We've made it through the invasion, but it's pretty obvious that the aftermath is going to be rough."

"A nightmare," Phil added.

"We don't know who or what has survived. We're going to have to get out there and explore," Pat said.

Andie turned her eyes back to the sky show. "It's going to be a world we've never seen. We've been so protected here in the park."

"True," said Phil. "The cities and suburbs probably don't exist anymore."

"I have to ask…why did your eyes turn red a few minutes ago? It's a dead giveaway that you're not totally human."

"It was an automatic response to signals the ships were sending each other. We never realized it would happen, and we're sorry for your scare," Pat replied.

"Are you like the skinny creatures with ovoid heads I saw at the cabin? They looked like insects, and they clicked their hands."

"No. Those are lesser beings from our planet who function as helpers to our race. They would never be able to enter a human's body. They do not have the flow of their form as we have," Phil said.

"Flow? Like shape-shifting?" Andie asked.

"No, we are more malleable, but we are always the same being."

"Okay," Andie breathed in deeply. There was so much information to absorb, so much more she wanted to know.

"What is the name of your planet?"

"What we call our planet cannot be translated into any of your languages here on Earth. I could give you a descriptive name but it still would not come close to the original meaning," Phil said.

"Are the other aliens from your planet going to come back?" Andie said.

"If mankind can do it right this time, and not ravage the Earth, then probably not," Phil said.

They watched the alien exodus for hours, laying in silence on the bare rocks that still held the warmth of the day. Andie had returned the gun to her waist pouch, but kept her hand close to the opening.

"I guess we'll tell our children about this someday," Andie mused.

"You certainly might. We, unfortunately, cannot have children," Phil said.

"I am worried about returning to towns and meeting other people. I keep thinking about those Mad Max movies. Some people might not be so nice after this experience," Pat said.

"We'll have to find a place where we can go and maybe settle down peacefully," said Phil.

"I'm hoping that there are rural areas with houses still standing," Andie said.

"It's a good thought. Hold on to it," Phil said.

The sun began to rise, and the darkness lifted. Where once there had been a sky full of alien technology, there were only a few motherships remaining. And then they too moved out of sight, back to the unknown reaches of space.

"I want to go home," said Andie

# CHAPTER 35

With the day shining upon them, Andie and the twins packed up the tent and any cooking materials they could carry. They hoped there was no longer any need to hide in the woods. They would descend the mountainside and make their way back to Andie's cabin.

Phil stood in the crushed grass where the tent had stood. "You know, I'm sort of going to miss this place."

"You're kidding, right?" asked Pat.

"On one hand it was a drudge-carrying water from the stream, cooking over a fire, cleaning clothes, freaking out over noises in the woods, hiding from our brothers…"

"But on the other hand, it was an adventure that we survived. I feel like we are our own heroes, in a sense."

Pat smirked. "Some heroes. We just went into hiding."

Phil grimaced. "True. But we hid well and now we can carry on. Millions died. We didn't. I think that makes us special."

Andie snorted her laugh. "Like being part alien isn't special enough?"

Pat slapped his brother on the back. "Okay, big hero, let's get out of here. I, for one, am glad to be out in broad daylight and away from this place."

They all carried jury-rigged packs on their back or chest in addition to their backpacks. It was a slow cautious walk down the trail. Andie slipped once on a pile of loose pebbles and ended up traveling several yards on her backside.

The guys helped her to regain her feet, since she felt like an unbalanced turtle with a shell on her front and back.

"You okay?" asked Phil.

Andie looked up at him through hair that had fallen over her eyes. "Everything is just fine, except my pride and my rear end." She rubbed her bottom to indicate her minor injury.

"Sorry. I can't help you with either," Phil said.

"Harumph."

They managed to complete their journey without another incident, although with the heat of the day bearing down, they were sweating through their shirts.

"Water break," Pat called.

They stopped close to Andie's familiar plateau, chugging from canteens and reused water bottles. After a long swig of the refreshing water, Andie commented, "We're about a half hour from my camp. Do you think we should spend the night there?"

Pat squinted into the distance, "Not sure. Let's see how we feel when we get there."

As they started to descend again, Andie pondered, "I can't stop thinking about the metal monsters. I'm hoping they went back to the spaceships. It would make our lives complicated if we had to keep dodging those things."

Phil nodded. "Right. I'm sure they were taken back with the ships. Our brothers were so thorough in their human clean-up operations I figure they wouldn't want to leave any of their stuff behind. I know that sounds convoluted…"

"No, I get it. It's like they're the intergalactic waste management company," Andie said.

"No trash left behind," added Pat. "Sorry, that was tasteless."

"I'm beyond that," Andie reassured him.

The group reached flat land and slashed their way through the tall grasses with their hands. "This is getting so thick," Phil noted.

"We must be approaching summer," Andie said. "Everything is growing like crazy."

As soon as they entered the meadow where the remains of the cabin sat teetering with its bent sides, Andie heard Satchmo's loud barks and whimpers. She dropped her packs where she was standing, then raced over to her car to find the bulldog. Satchmo was pulling at his rope, excited and eager to see his familiar human. Andie pulled him into her arms and kissed his wrinkled head.

"Hey, boy. It's me. I told you I'd come back. Let's get you off the leash." She untied the rope but made sure to hold the end, to keep Satchmo from running into the woods. "That's better, right, boy?"

Satch ran around the men's legs, getting the rope twisted and tangled every which way. They all laughed at the dog's antics and gave him the attention he craved and deserved.

"I'm going to get Satch some fresh water and food. Why don't you guys make yourselves comfortable for a while?"

Pat and Phil sauntered over to inspect the broken cabin, checking out its structural weakness and sharing ideas on how it could be fixed.

With the dog fed, Andie searched in the Rav 4 for some quick foods. She walked over to the men with a peanut butter jar, a tin of saltines and a can of Hawaiian Punch in her arms. She even had a can opener for the punch.

"A meal fit for a king," Phil laughed.

"Or an alien," said Andie.

"I wonder if you'll ever get over that?" asked Pat.

"I doubt it," said Andie.

The brothers exchanged glances then sat down to partake of the light repast. Even Satchmo had a few crackers with peanut butter, which of course, made them laugh as the dog tried to open his mouth to chew.

"Okay," Pat said, as he wiped crumbs from his hands, "Now it's time to make some decisions."

Andie felt her heart sink. She wanted to go home, but she also didn't want to leave the cabin area. Joe was buried there.

"Ah, do you think the cabin can be salvaged?" she asked.

Pat nodded, "Sure. If that's what you want. But Phil and I were thinking that we want to leave the park as soon as possible. What are your thoughts?"

Andie looked around the meadow, at the timbers of the cabin, at the steady roaring stream, at Joe's grave and its shovel marker. She would find it hard to leave after so much that had happened here. But she knew it was time to go.

"When are we leaving?" she asked.

The men sprang to their feet, and pulled Andie to stand next to them.

"Now!" said Pat.

"Right this minute," Phil agreed.

"Okay," Pat said, "What can we do here? Phil and I can hike up to our car, but we figured that we need to get your vehicle moving first."

"We'll have to pull off all the camouflage," Andie said, already racing over to her car. She pushed off branches, vines and leaves, exposing the front of the Rav 4. With the help of the men, the car was uncovered and all the detritus was removed from behind the car. Andie got into the driver's seat and backed the car out of the woods, as Phil directed her movements and Pat held Satchmo at bay. She parked the car in front of the cabin and hopped out.

"That felt so good, to be in the driver's seat again. I have a nearly full tank, and I'm ready to go. We'll need to clear some brush from the road up to

Skyline Drive, but it shouldn't be too bad," Andie said.

"Okay, let's put our backpacks into your car, then we'll walk ahead of your car as beaters," Pat said. They loaded their equipment and Satchmo into the Rav.

"Hey, Satch!" Andie rubbed his head. "You ready?" Satch barked, and Andie put her car into low gear to make the climb up the ragged pathway. The men grabbed any large tree branches that might impede the car's progress, and Andie drove around any questionable areas. They reached Skyline Drive, and Andie felt like shouting in relief. She rolled down her window and called out, "Get in! I'll take you to your car."

The guys climbed in, with Phil up front, Pat squeezed into the back, and Satchmo in the passenger seat foot well once again. Andie drove slow on the road, scanning for anything unusual or moving. She drove to the edge of the tunnel and turned off the car. "Now what?" she asked.

"Now we take our cars back to whatever civilization there might be. You can follow us in the Rav."

"But where to? What direction?" asked Andie.

"We want to go back to our hometown, in Missouri," Phil said without meeting her eyes.

"I see," said Andie quietly. "And I want to go to my home in Maryland. I need to see what's left, if anything."

They sat in silence for a few moments, then Andie said, "Why can't we do both? My home in Columbia is only ninety minutes away. We can check out the situation there, and then move on to Missouri."

"It's about fourteen hours from Columbia to our home in Missouri. We can do it in a few days drive, depending," said Phil.

"It's not a bad idea to go somewhere close for tonight to regroup, think through our plans. Who knows what we'll find on the highway once we get out of the park at Front Royal," Pat said.

"Agreed," said Phil. "Will you be okay driving alone with Satchmo?" he asked Andie with concern etched into his kind face.

"I'll be tailing you guys like a fly on honey," she said. "I know you'll have more room in your car than you would have in here with all my supplies."

"Our phones aren't working so we'll wave our arms out the window and beep if we want to stop along the way," said Pat.

"Okay," said Andie. "Let's saddle up and ride."

"Let's go!" said Phil as the brothers ran to their car. They took a few minutes to move things around and then let the engine run after sitting in the tunnel for a few weeks. When they pulled out of the tunnel, with Phil driving, they drove a short way past Andie, then did a U-turn to head north. She waved as they drove by, then pulled out behind them.

"I hope this isn't the biggest mistake I've ever made," she said aloud to herself.

# *CHAPTER 36*

The return drive through Shenandoah National Park was stranger than strange. There were no cars, no people, no structures. It was as if they were the only ones who were privileged to be in the magnificence of the wilderness and mountains. Andie averted her eyes from where the Skyland Hotel once stood, where the aliens had blasted the place into ash. She didn't need to ruminate on what once was. There would be time for that later, maybe, after she had found a place to live and settled down. She knew that she carried Joe in her heart and always would. She would also carry Miss Bey, a great and colorful woman.

After making the gate at Front Royal, Andie followed the men's car on to Highway 95 North. There were cars scattered here and there on the road, but for the most part the way was oddly clear. Andie thought that the rolling tripods had blasted any obstacles in their path. It was efficient, she supposed, but ruthless.

There were enough cars left so that the survivors would be able to access gas when they needed it. She wondered if gas evaporated after a while. She figured that it got sludgy eventually. Their resources would dwindle over time.

They passed exits for major towns along the way, but saw no tall buildings which once marked their existence. There were no longer any rest stops, no golden arches in the distance. Andie began feeling nervous. How was she going to live in this desolate world?

Not a single person was in sight. Andie knew that she and the twin brothers could not be the only ones alive. She kept alert trying to scan both sides of the road for any others, but she never saw even one straggler. Perhaps the survivors are still hiding, she thought. Perhaps they aren't sure that the aliens have left. And perhaps they were afraid of who their fellow survivors might be. Andie began to feel exposed in her car, traveling the open roads without protection.

The twins beeped and waved in front of her after an hour. She drifted over to the parking lane and turned the key in the ignition. She closed her eyes and took a huge gulp of air. She hadn't realized how tense she was. Satchmo gave a short bark, and Andie jerked in her seat.

As she got out of the car and opened the passenger door to let Satchmo out for a walk, she surveyed the landscape of trees and plants. Phil joined her as she viewed the surrounding area. "It has changed, hasn't it?" he said. "No more signs of industry. It's just the Earth as it once was before humans grew too big for their britches."

Andie nodded. "Yes, I suppose so. Hopefully, there are some places for humans left."

"I'm sure there will be, once we get to suburbia. A lot of people escaped in the opening days of the invasion, but I'll bet a lot of people held on in the suburbs, unless the aliens blasted their way inside. And, unfortunately, those people who didn't leave were flushed out when their resources ran dry. Being without water and food are going to make people leave the comfort of their homes."

Andie nodded, then pulled on Satch's rope. "Let's go, boy. Gotta see what's left at home."

The remainder of the trip was quiet. And then they hit Reston, Virginia. Or rather, the area that once was Reston, Virginia. Andie and Pat stopped the cars when the fields of devastation spread out before them, a grey wasteland of ash several inches deep that spread across and almost covered the road. There was nothing to see for miles to the East and to the North. The once bustling metropolis was now a flat alien landscape that seemed to offer up the cries of the countless dead when the winds blew across the barren fields. Andie opened her car door, in total disbelief and shock at the remnants of a once-vital city. She stumbled a few feet, then slid to her knees in the dust. She held her hands in prayer and began to speak.

"Bless the people of this land, and all the lands of our world, who came together to live in harmony and fellowship. They worked hard to create lives that were meaningful and good. It is our fault, and the fault of our leaders, that we have ruined our planet. The skies, the seas, and the land were all victims of our desire for better and easier ways of living. Instead of working with our resources, we worked against them. This ruined land is the price we had to pay. The aliens destroyed us so that we would not completely destroy Earth. For the very few of us that are survivors, we still have a chance to make amends and begin new ways of living. I will try my hardest to be a protector of Earth. I thank the universe that my life has been spared."

Andie stood and wiped the dust from her knees. She felt reborn amidst the devastation. The struggles, the pain, the exhaustion had all led her to this moment of raw commitment. There was no going back to a way of life that allowed her to ignore the repercussions of wasteful and unthinking actions.

Andie turned and saw Phil and Pat both kneeling in the dust. Were they, too, having their own epiphanies, even though they were only half humans? She probably would never know, but she respectfully turned away to give them privacy. She felt bereft, but empowered by her new beliefs.

Andie got into her Rav, and the boys slipped into their own car shortly thereafter. When Andie followed the other car the rest of the way on Route 95 and then to the Route 32 exit for Columbia, her heart began to pound. On this road, she could see homes through the trees, although she couldn't tell their condition.

As she drove on to Broken Land Parkway, just a few miles from her home, she began to weep. The town looked the same. Aside from the many blown out windows in houses and apartment buildings, it seemed untouched from the fire of the aliens' weapons. She signaled to the guys that she would be pulling ahead of them for the final drive. She drove around cars parked in the road. The trees were full of bright green leaves, and the slight winds rustled the branches. As she turned on to her roadway into her apartment complex, she felt numb. Joe had lived here. Miss Bey had lived here, too. She parked her car in front of her building and walked with Satchmo to her front door. She had kept her keys, and now she retrieved them from her pocket. As she turned the silver key in the lock and opened the door, Pat and Phil stood behind her.

Her apartment was quite warm and even a bit musty smelling. She walked over to the blinds and opened them wide so that the light could pour in. She opened the sliding glass doors and stood on her deck, overlooking the small patch of woods. She could see cardinals darting among the branches; she could hear the songbirds hiding in the leaves.

"There's no place like home," Andie said as she turned to face the men.

"I'm glad its still here for you," Phil said with a soft smile.

"We can definitely stay here tonight," Pat said. "I know I'm too tired to continue on the road. That crater that once was Reston sure took it out of me, and no doubt there are a lot more shocking things to see as we head west."

"I think that makes three of us," said Andie. She flipped a switch but no lights came on. She wasn't really expecting the electricity to work but habits die hard. "Good thing we brought water with us."

"Let's get what we need from the car," Pat motioned to Phil. "We'll bring your backpack," he indicated to Andie.

"Thanks," she said. She heard the guys calling out as they walked to the parking lot. "Hey!'" they called. "Yoo-hoo, anyone here?" She walked to her bedroom and viewed the unmade bed. "No time like the present," she said as she began ripping off wrinkled sheets. She had clean sheets in the closet, and she was determined to use them. As she tugged on the fitted sheet, one corner being difficult as usual, she heard a sound at her doorway.

"Andie?" the voice tentatively asked.

She whipped around, and there stood Frank Terranova, the Howard County police officer.

"Oh, my God!" she cried. "I can't believe you're alive!"

She threw down the sheets and ran over to Frank. She hugged him with every last strength in her being. The sight of his familiar face overwhelmed her. "How are you still here? And, why are you here?"

Frank rumbled with laughter, then held her away, inspecting her face, her lean body, her tousled hair. "You are a sight for sore eyes. I don't believe it."

"Are there others?" Andie asked, her words tumbling from her lips. "I mean, here in Columbia. Are there people that made it?"

"Not many," Frank answered. "Not many at all. I routinely check all the apartment complexes and houses in this area, but most people fled in the beginning, when the discs were hunting us down. When I come through this complex, I always stop by your building to see if you'd come back. I just had a feeling that you would. Maybe it was wishful thinking, but look, here you are."

Andie looked into his dark brown eyes. She was relieved that he had been spared the fate of so many others. She had known he was a decent man from just the few encounters she had with him, and maybe now she could get to know him even better. In this new world, one could never have enough friends. Of course, she would have to process the time that she and Joe had shared and also the grief that she now carried within her. However, she knew she would be open to exploring a new friendship with Frank.

Suddenly, Satchmo was at their feet, barking at Frank.

"Down, Satch," Andie ordered. "He's a friend."

Satchmo backed off but stood watching Andie and Frank.

"I met your other friends outside," Frank said, "The twins. They told me that they were with you. They said 'Andie', and I just knew it had to be you."

"Yes, Pat and Phil," she said. "I met them in the mountains. You're not going to believe what's up with them."

"Oh? They seem like nice guys. What happened to the people you left with?" Frank's forehead crinkled as he questioned her.

"That's a story for another day," Andie answered. She looked at Frank and pressed her lips together. She would tell him everything, of course, but right now it was too much, too soon.

She sucked in her lower lip, and asked, "So, how do you feel about Missouri?"

"Missouri?" Frank chuckled, "Um, Missouri sounds good. I mean, they were known for their beer there."

Andie nodded with a mischievous light beginning to show in her eyes, "Yes, Missouri did have beer before the aliens came. It also had great parks. And the twins want to go there because it was their home, and I was thinking of going with them. So, I wondered if maybe, sorta, kinda, you'd like to come, too?"

"Are you flirting with me, Andie?" Frank asked.

"Maybe," she admitted. "A little bit. I just really would like you to come."

Satchmo barked from where he had been watching them.

Andie bent down and picked up the old dog. "Yes, Satch, you're coming, too. That's cause you're my best boy." She hugged him to her.

Satchmo licked Andie's face.

Andie turned back to Frank and asked, "So, what's the verdict?"

Frank smiled. "I'm coming with you."

Andie held Satchmo even tighter to her chest, and the surprised dog gave her a yelp in response.

"That's great," Andie said. "Now I have two questions for you."

"What? There's a test for going to Missouri?"

Andie laughed and tilted her head. "Do you happen to read science fiction? And do you like dogs?"

# *Acknowledgments*

Books need people. They need writers and editors who will find the mistakes and offer suggestions for improvement. This book had talented Beta readers who gave me unflinching critiques and offered imaginative ideas. Thank you to Lorraine Anderson, Susan Olesen, Lisa Sponaugle and Cynthia Woods for their time and invaluable assistance. I'd also like to thank Steven Wilson who published my previous books under his Firebringer imprint and encouraged me in the publication of this novel. Special thanks also need to be extended to Phillip Duff who gave me the idea of why the aliens came to destroy humankind over drinks during a convention at the Hunt Valley Inn. Lastly and forever, thanks to my dear friend, Bonnie Leroy, who truly believed in the existence of aliens.

*Diane Lee Baron*
*February 7, 2023*

www.ingramcontent.com/pod-product-compliance
Lightning Source LLC
LaVergne TN
LVHW020606160826
845677LV00020B/2944

* 9 7 9 8 9 8 7 9 7 1 1 9 2 *